Praise for the Puzzle Train

"It is very exciting and I'm sorry the programme doesn't exist on TV," – Jess aged 10

"I loved the Puzzle Train. Tom and his friends are a lively bunch and I found myself cheering them on. The puzzles are challenging and exciting. The story is an adventure and a fun read. I can't wait for the next one," – Mandy

"So good, I couldn't put it down and spent the whole evening reading it," – Amelia aged 12

"I enjoyed the easy reading of the Puzzle Train … the puzzles were cleverly constructed and I shared the feelings of dread and anticipation of the puzzleteers … I found the story compelling," – Maree

"Gripping. It kept me hooked from page 1. Who is the Conductor … ?" – Gabriella aged 11

PUZZLE TRAIN

Richard James Edwards

PUZZLE TRAIN

Beyond The Vale Publishing

Writing a book is a lot about one man sitting in front of a laptop, but it takes a support network of people to bring it together. Fortunately, I have an amazing support network. Debz, without whom this book would have never been written in the first place and Isabelle who makes me proud and provides inspiration. It wouldn't be the book it is without the support and guidance of Sandy, Mandy and John.

Thank you all.

Puzzle (noun)

1. a game, toy, or problem designed to test ingenuity or
    knowledge.

2. a person or thing that is difficult to understand or explain; an
    enigma

Chapter 1 - Carriage Six

Tom gripped the threadbare arms of his favorite chair and stared, unblinking, at the screen. Tuesday evening was Puzzle Train evening and had been for as long as he could remember. There had never been a winner, but tonight could be the night.

He had lived every moment of the last five carriages with the six contestants, the puzzleteers. He had analyzed the Conductor's poems, the vital clues at the beginning of each carriage that were needed to solve the puzzles within; tried to warn the puzzleteers of the traps that awaited them; and leapt with joy each time they progressed to the next carriage. Now he was willing them to solve carriage six. The final carriage. If they solved this before the train arrived at its destination then they would have ten extra minutes to attempt the puzzle that would earn them the reward – the station puzzle.

Tom urged them on.

"You need to crack the anagrams," he shouted at the TV.

Only eight teams in the eleven years the Puzzle Train had been running had made it to the station puzzle. The Puzzle Train was the same age as Tom.

Those eight teams that had made it to the station puzzle had all failed to complete the final challenge. No-one had ever won the grand prizes of five-million-dollars and a meeting with the Conductor.

"Build the blocks and match the patterns! Geez!" He covered his eyes with his hands, peering through his fingers as on screen two puzzleteers were staring with vacant expressions at the plastic blocks in front of them.

Tom grabbed his phone. He and best friend Isabelle had been messaging throughout the show so far, as they did on every Tuesday evening when they watched the Puzzle Train.

"They're going to do it. 18 minutes left to complete carriage 6." Tom typed at speed, eyes flicking between the TV and his phone. He didn't want to miss a second of the show, but this was big. Huge. It had to be shared. Ninety minutes to complete a puzzle in each of six carriages. They were ahead of schedule entering the final carriage. This hardly ever happened. "And there's still 3 puzzleteers left."

Six puzzleteers started each episode. There were many booby traps in each carriage, and the Conductor just loved to catch a careless puzzleteer in a cage. Tom suspected that sometimes he would just cage a contestant because he didn't like them, they weren't trying hard enough or even just for his own amusement. They would receive a five, ten or fifteen minute punishment depending on what they had done to earn the cage. The

Conductor would then appear as a silhouette on the carriage wall just to mock them.

Three had been trapped in earlier carriages despite Tom's shouted warnings. The rest of the team could have waited for them, but not this team. That was exactly the kind of ruthlessness that Tom believed would see them through carriage six.

"If they get through the station puzzle, they get to meet the Conductor. Finally, we'll find out who he is!" He typed a second message to Isabelle. As he glanced at the timer on the screen. Twelve minutes to go.

His phone buzzed. He glanced down at it. "Then you'll stop obsessing with who he is," teased Isabelle.

Tom's fixation with the Conductor had driven most of his school mates nuts. Even Isabelle, who was also a huge fan of the Puzzle Train, got irritated with him sometimes. Tom needed to know who he was. He didn't know why, but he had to know.

He was pleased Phil, his stepfather, wasn't at home. He seemed to have a strange hatred for the quiz show, and the Conductor in particular. He flew into a rage if he found Tom watching it or if he even mentioned it. Unpleasant arguments about Tom's grades nearly always followed.

Tom thought hard, back to the poem for carriage six. 'The clue is always in the poem'. Tom's gran's voice came in his head as it often did. She was his favorite person in the whole world. She used to let him stay up past his bedtime when he was younger so they could watch the Puzzle Train together.

Tom wished he could be in the carriage, imagining his gran watching at home cheering him on. The show was for grown-ups only. He couldn't understand how dumb the adults were sometimes, when he and Isabelle could solve the clues!

A heated discussion between the three remaining puzzleteers was starting on the screen.

"Don't argue," called Tom. Arguments nearly always ended in someone doing something rash and being caught in a cage.

"But I think we have to build the patterns from the blocks." Jim, the one remaining male puzzleteer waved his arms around.

"Yes, yes, yes!' shouted Tom. "He's right, listen to him." Why were they taking so long to work it out?

"Phew!" exhaled Tom as - argument avoided - the other two puzzleteers, Amelia and Melissa, agreed and they all jumped into action. "Let's get going, then. This time will go quickly."

"Finally!" Tom clapped. He looked at the timer in the corner of the screen, there were only nine minutes left. "Quickly," he urged.

Tom tapped a message to Isabelle. "Those letters on the blocks must have something to do with the password."

"These patterns are too similar." On screen, Jim scratched his head as he frowned at a block. He picked up a second block.

"Come on, Jim. Carriage six. Get a move on," urged Melissa as she walked past with a block in each hand.

"Don't lose it now, Jim." Tom stamped his feet on the floor.

"This is impossible. Look at them." He held the blocks out to Melissa. "They're almost identical." He tossed them on the floor.

"It's not supposed to be easy, Jim. This is carriage six," Tom advised.

"Jim! Focus!" Melissa scolded him.

"These blocks have letters on, we'll be able to get the password from these." Melissa waved the blocks in Jim's face.

"Yes! Build the patterns. Write the letters on the board, get the password. Come on!" Tom jumped up and shouted at his TV.

"We need the password and we'll get it from these letters," Melissa snapped at Jim.

"That's what I just said!" Tom was wide-eyed in his living room. They still had time, they could still defeat carriage six. "Yes, that's what the Conductor means by 'mix' from the poem. They'll have to rearrange some words."

"Give me that!" All of a sudden, Amelia's frustration boiled over and she snatched at the block Melissa was holding. Melissa didn't let go of the block. For a second, the two women both pulled the block until Amelia's hand slipped. She lost her balance and tripped over the pile of five blocks she had been working on and thumped on the floor on her bottom.

"Hey!" shouted Amelia, from the carriage floor. "What d'you think you're doing? I needed that." She stood up and glared at Melissa.

"Don't do it!" Tom covered his eyes.

Station Master Marvin, host of the show, often popped up on screen when something interesting was happening to offer a comment, word of advice or a bad joke. He echoed Tom's concerns.

"Oh dear, they're going to run out of time if they start arguing. There're still lots of other blocks, Melissa, use the other blocks."

Marvin's words were for the audience at home only though, they were never broadcast inside the carriage.

"I need that one," Amelia said through gritted teeth. "Look, it forms part of my pattern." She snatched the block back.

"Stop!" Jim turned around from looking at his blocks to see the two women glaring at each other. Amelia angry, Melissa defiant.

"Calm down. The Conductor's trying to get in your head," Tom implored.

"Give it back. I need it for my pattern," Melissa shouted.

Amelia turned her back.

Melissa grabbed her by the shoulder. "Give it to me!"

"Stop!" pleaded Jim.

"Stop!" Tom called from his living room.

"Stop!" The deep booming voice of the Conductor filled the carriage and rumbled through the speakers of Tom's TV.

The carriage was plunged into darkness, a red flashing light appeared above the exit door and a siren sounded which was so loud the puzzleteers dropped their blocks and covered their ears. Instantly a cage dropped from the ceiling and trapped Melissa. On the carriage wall next to the whiteboard appeared the number five in red, stretching from the ceiling to the floor. It ticked down to 4:59.

"I knew that was going to happen!" Tom called out to his mom as she walked past the living room. He put his head in his hands. "They'll never complete this puzzle now."

The siren stopped, the lights went back on and the puzzleteers looked around to see Melissa looking furious, rattling the bars of the cage. Tom knew, as everyone who watched the Puzzle Train knew, the cages were utterly immovable.

The Conductor's silhouette appeared on the carriage wall. Normally he laughed when he trapped someone. This time he was angry.

"No fighting on my train!"

Melissa looked at him from the cage and must have said something pretty bad as the only sound coming from Tom's TV now was a long string of 'beeps'.

"Five minutes for you to calm down," the Conductor's voice filled the carriage. "The minimum amount of time, because until then you were performing well."

The Conductor's silhouette disappeared from the wall.

Marvin was watching the action from the corner of the screen. "She was lucky. I've seen the Conductor give ten minutes, or sometimes even fifteen minutes for similar events."

Tom agreed with Marvin.

"Are you questioning me?" The Conductor's silhouette appeared in the opposite corner. His voice rumbled through the TV speakers.

"N-n-no, Conductor. Of course not." Marvin's smile faltered.

The Conductor would often tell Marvin off. Tom was sure the Conductor and Marvin were really friends off-screen. Well he hoped so, anyway.

Tom stared at the Conductor until he disappeared, looking for any clue to his identity. "Who are you?" He wouldn't pause or rewind the show while he was watching. The thought that Isabelle would know the outcome before he did put him off.

Melissa being caged spurred Jim and Amelia into action.

"Yes!" Tom cheered as the puzzleteers completed the first anagram. "Quickly! You still have eight minutes."

Anagrams two and three quickly followed. The two remaining puzzleteers worked fast, cheered on by Melissa.

"Seven left. Then they can get the password." Tom was biting his nails.

With three minutes to go, the cage disappeared into the ceiling and Melissa leapt into action. Jim and Amelia had completed another four anagrams.

"Three anagrams, three minutes." Tom was on the edge of his seat, fixed on the action in front of him.

"Two more," he whispered, watching through his fingers.

"One to go!" He jumped up and was directing the three puzzleteers. Just fifteen seconds remained.

"Yes!" yelled Melissa. "I know what the password is!" She tapped the word into a keyboard attached to the side wall.

"That's it, that's right!" Tom was jumping up and down. "Ten seconds left. Get the key! GET THE KEY!"

Above Melissa's head, a glass bowl containing the key tipped slowly over. The key to exit carriage six.

Melissa held her hand out to catch the key. Six seconds, five, four.

The key landed in her palm and she sprinted from one end of the carriage to the other. "Out the way!" she screamed to Jim and Amelia.

"Come on! You can do it," shouted Tom, still jumping up and down, his eyes glued to the screen.

Three seconds, two. Melissa fumbled the key in the lock. Frantically she tried to open the door. One, zero. A siren filled the carriage, the door was still locked shut.

"No!" Tom threw his head back and buried his face in his hands. "No! they were so close!" he yelled at the TV.

Tom slumped back on his chair, his heart began to return to its normal speed, as on the screen the shot had cut to the six puzzleteers on the platform, with the beige carriages of the Puzzle

Train behind them. They were being interviewed by Station Master Marvin, who was, as usual, wearing a brightly colored suit and was full of excitement to hear their stories from the train.

Marvin turned from the puzzleteers to look directly at the camera. "Thanks for watching. Before I say TTFN," – Marvin always finished each episode saying 'Ta Ta For Now' – "I have a very special announcement. Some of you may know that the Puzzle Train has been running for eleven years. And is nearly five hundred episodes old. To celebrate we have some very special episodes planned. We will be welcoming back some old puzzleteers. We have a few celebrities to take on the train for charity, but first" …he paused for dramatic effect … "as a thank you to all our young, loyal fans, we have news of a children's special!"

"What?" said Tom, eyes widening.

"Is there anyone out there between the ages of ten and twelve? Yes, you!" He pointed at the camera. "You look clever. How old are you? Have you ever wanted to take part in the Puzzle Train?"

Tom was sure his heart skipped a beat, dislodged itself from his chest and leapt into his throat. "Yes, Marvin. More than anything!"

"Great, I knew it. I could tell." Marvin beamed at the camera.

"Our children's special is going to be aaaa-mazing! We just don't have any children at the moment, which is going to make it slightly difficult." Marvin pointed at screen again. "But you! Yes, you! You could be the solution. You could be joining me here." Marvin held his arms out, as the camera panned back to show the platform and the carriages behind.

"If you want to attempt our puzzles," he said, spinning around on the spot, "then apply on our website. The address is on screen now." Tom knew it off by heart, having visited it on many occasions.

"Applications close on Thursday at 6 pm. That's right, only two days to apply. The first winner will be announced on our website on Friday!"

Tom's hands were shaking in excitement as he grabbed his phone and messaged Isabelle. "A children's special! I've got to get on that!"

He got up to run to his bedroom, almost crashing into Phil, his stepfather, on the way.

"Where are you going?" growled Phil, his face full of thunder.

"Upstairs." Tom tried to push past, but Phil blocked his way.

"I heard from your history teacher again today. I want a word with you."

Tom swallowed hard, this was not going to be good.

Below is the full puzzle from last night's carriage six. Tom was right, it's all about anagrams. Can you rearrange the letters to make eight words? Then take the letter as indicated (for example, from 'crocodile' take the third letter) and rearrange those nine letters into the password which would have taken the team through to the station puzzle.

									Take letter:
Rearrange the letters	R D I C E L O O C *c r o c o d i l e*								3
Rearrange the letters	N I O D E U T A C								3
Rearrange the letters	N N N I I G G E B								5
Rearrange the letters	L T N I E D I A C								7
Rearrange the letters	G K C A P N I A G								7
Rearrange the letters	B M C E A L N U E								2
Rearrange the letters	J C E V E I A D T								6
Rearrange the letters	H O M E S T G N I								3
Rearrange the letters	D D N E E W Y S A								9
Put the password here									

Chapter 2 – To Apply or not to Apply?

"Did you apply?" Isabelle asked without even a 'hello' as she met Tom at the large tree in the corner of the playground.

Tom shook his head sadly and looked up through the canopy leaves to the blue sky beyond.

"I thought you would be the first to apply." Isabelle frowned, but then the reason dawned on her. "Phil?"

"He turned the WiFi off and grounded me," Tom muttered.

He thumped the back of his head on the tree then looked around the playground where groups of children were gathering, relaxing, chatting or playing sports. Tom wondered how many of them had applied last night.

"You didn't get chance to apply then? As soon as Marvin announced the children's episode last night I was straight onto my laptop."

"No," mumbled Tom as he fought against the lump in his throat.

Isabelle put a hand on his shoulder. "What happened with Phil this time?" She could see a moistening around his eyes.

"I would have told you if you answered your phone," Tom's voice was cracking.

"Sorry, Tom. Dad and I were watching a documentary after I finished my application."

Tom couldn't imagine watching a documentary with Phil.

"It was Griffon. He's got it in for me. He doesn't pick on any of the rest of the history class like he picks on me."

"Detention again?"

Tom swallowed hard, still trying to clear the lump in his throat. "Yup. No internet for a week."

The bell rang and Tom and Isabelle went to their separate classes. Tom tried to pay attention but found his gaze wandering towards the window. Back to last night's Puzzle Train and Marvin's announcement.

"Tell me about the qualification puzzles," Tom blurted out as soon as he met up with Isabelle at lunch break.

Isabelle knew Tom's obsession with the show better than anyone, except for his gran. Often, it led to a great deal of teasing from their fellow students. She had been expecting a barrage of questions.

"Well, according to the website, there are twenty different puzzles and the system will randomly allocate you three of them."

"Oh, I wonder why they do that."

"I guess it's so you can't copy someone else's answers."

"That makes sense. So what puzzles did you get?"

"In the first puzzle I had to rearrange some letters to make different words about the show, like Conductor, Marvin, Train and other words like that. Random letters would run across the screen. There was a really tough time limit. I only just made it in time."

"That doesn't sound too bad."

"Then there was a really hard 'spot the difference'."

"What was so hard about it?"

"There was such a lot of detail in the pictures. They were dark and there was only a small circle of light which shifted as you moved the mouse over the picture."

"And the last puzzle?"

"It was like a jigsaw puzzle. The picture was the train and the carriages, but if you moved a piece to the wrong spot, all the pieces jumped out of the picture and you had to start from the beginning."

"Sounds easy enough."

"They were fine. The really tricky bit is the tie-break question. Describe a day in the Conductor's life in no more than one hundred words."

Tom looked at her. "But no one even knows who he is. The most secretive man on TV."

There was much speculation all over the internet about who the Conductor was. Tom had spent many hours of fruitless research trying to find out more about him. The Conductor was the brains behind the show and had been since it started, eleven years ago. He never showed his face. Appearing only as a silhouette sitting behind a desk to mock an unlucky contestant who had become caught in a cage for incurring his displeasure.

Theories were boundless as to who he was. Footballer, newsreader, politician, astronaut, movie star and some speculation he was even a former president. Tom lapped them all up. He studied the brimmed-hat silhouette in every episode for a clue that would lead to his identity.

Former Puzzle Train employees were always swooped on by the media, but apart from speculation, the Conductor's identity was a secret, even from them.

"That's why the question is so brilliant," smiled Isabelle.

"Can you imagine what it would be like to be on the train, Issy?" Tom's eyes were growing wide at the prospect. "I really thought last night's team were going to do it."

"They should have made it through to the station puzzle," Isabelle agreed. "They had eighteen minutes to complete carriage six."

"You know only eight teams have ever made it to the station puzzle," Tom added hurriedly. "Eight. In nearly five hundred episodes. The Conductor is a genius."

"Yes, you've told me at least a million times. Is that why you're so desperate to meet him? Because he's a genius?"

Tom frowned, deep in thought. Why was he bursting to know who the Conductor was? It was deep-rooted in him. He just had to know.

Isabelle knew Tom well enough to tell that an answer was unlikely to come, so she continued. "And isn't seventy-two minutes …"

"… the third quickest time for the first five carriages," Tom continued, finishing her sentence. He couldn't contain himself. The chance to quote a Puzzle Train statistic snapped him from his thoughts. "I knew the final carriage was about anagrams as soon as the poem clue mentioned the carriage was in a mix."

"It was that guy's fault. Jim. He started the argument," said Isabelle.

Tom knew that the Conductor enjoyed designing puzzles with hidden twists in them. The Conductor liked logic and team work.

"Melissa deserved the cage. But it cost them," he reasoned. His gaze drifted before snapping back into focus. After the Conductor's identity, the technology that powered the cages was the next biggest secret. They always dropped exactly where they were needed from the ceiling, leaving no trace. They were always the right size for the puzzleteer and always firmly fixed to the floor. Not even the strongest puzzleteer could move them.

"How awesome would it be to meet the Conductor and win five million dollars, Issy?"

Isabelle couldn't help but agree. The biggest un-won cash prize in TV history.

"We need it right now, Issy. The house is falling apart and mom's working herself crazy. New house, new car, new start. Vacation would be nice. I haven't seen gran in months, since she moved to the coast. Maybe we could even get away from Phil."

"But he's your stepfather. It's such a shame you can't get along."

"He's an idiot. What mom ever saw in him is beyond me. It was a real struggle before he came along but things just feel worse now."

"Your mom loves him. You should accept that. And accept him." Isabelle finally snapped. All too often Tom moaned and complained about his home life.

"They're not even married," Tom countered. "How much can she love him? I just have to call him my stepfather because mom thinks we seem more of a family that way."

They glared at each other and were both relieved when the bell rang for start of afternoon classes.

They walked back to the main school building and were about to go their separate ways.

"I'm only trying to help," said Isabelle. "You can't wallow in self-pity all your life."

Tom looked at the steely expression on Isabelle's face. "I know. But I've got a plan to get mom and I out of this mess. After school I'm going to apply and win my place on the Puzzle Train. Hello the Conductor and five million. Goodbye Phil!"

Had an afternoon ever passed so slowly? Tom couldn't help but wonder. Was that clock stopped? Was it running backwards? Science class was not holding Tom's attention. His focus was on getting home and applying for the Puzzle Train.

Finally, the bell rang. There was a loud scrape of chairs as Tom and his fellow students fought to get out of class quickest. At the school gate, he found Isabelle waiting for him.

"Hi, Tom, how was your afternoon?"

She really enjoys school, thought Tom. Girls are weird.

"I thought it would never end," he said as they turned to walk in the direction of home. "All I want to do is get home and apply for the show before it's too late."

"Won't Phil have the internet turned off still?" asked Isabelle.

"It's okay. He won't be home until late, and I memorised the password." He quickened his pace.

"So, you can learn things when you're interested in them," Isabelle skipped to keep up.

Soon, they stopped outside Isabelle's house and said goodbye.

"I'll drop you a message to let you know how I get on," Tom turned to walk home.

"We're going out for dad's birthday this evening. We're going somewhere nice." She screwed up her face. "I'd rather just go for pizza. And no phones. Adults are so strange some times. But I'll definitely reply when I get home," she added as she waved and went inside.

Tom hurried home. He had plenty of time before Phil got home but it would be better to log on as soon as possible just in case.

Ugh, Phil. Mr. Angrypants. Tom was used to Phil being cross with him, but now he seemed grumpy with his mom as well.

"Give him a break," his mom told him after a particularly heated argument. "He's got this great new job, but there's loads of stress with it. He'll calm down."

Tom couldn't see what was so great about it if it made him so stressed. He had discussed it with his gran on the phone.

"You spend most of your day at work, a great job should be one you love," his gran had told him.

"I'm sure Phil doesn't love this job, otherwise why would he be so irritable all the time?" Tom replied. "And he hates the Puzzle Train. He's always saying the Conductor is an arrogant stuck up good for nothing."

"The Conductor loves his job. He obviously has brought out the worst in Phil."

"I must check out train tickets. I'd love to visit gran for the summer," Tom muttered to himself as he turned into his street. He looked down the row of driveways and was relieved to see no cars parked outside his house. Great. Peace and quiet to prepare my application, he thought.

He unlocked the door and shouldered it open, the door sticking against the frame. He flicked peeling paint off his shirt, heaved the door shut and ran to the living room. He switched the Wi-Fi router on and then ran straight up the stairs to his bedroom.

He was finally going to complete his application form. The thought gave him butterflies in his stomach.

The butterflies turned to stone when he switched on his laptop and saw that Phil had changed the Wi-Fi password. With Isabelle out for the evening there was no way he could think of to apply. When his mom came home, she didn't know what the new password was either. Phil worked until late and wouldn't reply to any messages. Dejected and upset, Tom went to bed determined to think of how he could get on the Puzzle Train website.

The thought struck him on the walk into school the next morning. He would go to the school library at lunch time and use the computers there. He met Isabelle at the school gates before his first class of the day and told her his plan.

"I can't believe Phil changed the password." Isabelle shook her head. "He really doesn't want you to apply."

Tom tried to contain his bitterness, but failed as he threw the door to the school building open with a slam.

"Using the library computers is a good idea. Are you sure the site isn't blocked by the school firewall."

"No, Issy. I've been on there before."

"When did you ever go to the library?" Isabelle raised her eyebrows. "Do you even know where it is?"

Tom tried to look offended, but had to concede his trips to the library were few and far between.

"You were at gymnastics camp last month and it was raining so I went in there. They're ancient computers and slow, but I was able to get on the Puzzle Train website."

"Well good luck. I'm working on advanced mathematics with Mr. Archer." Isabelle gave him the thumbs up as they headed to their different classrooms.

Tom willed the time to count down throughout the morning's lessons, and finally when the bell rang for the start of lunchtime, he packed his school bag quickly and sprinted down the hall to the library.

He barged the door open, earning a disapproving look from Mrs Stokes the librarian.

"Quiet," she snapped.

Mrs Stokes was fondly known throughout the school as the book dragon, her sharp features, long face and pointed nose left many younger students cowering behind the shelves. She seemed to have hawk-like vision and bat-like hearing, and ran the library with military precision and discipline. Her ability to breathe fire was just a rumor. "You'd better behave," she told him looking over her half-moon glasses.

"Sorry," Tom muttered and looked around the shelves stacked high with books for the computers.

He walked as quickly and quietly as he could to the far corner where there were three computers in a line on top of three desks.

Tom sat on a threadbare chair, wiggled the mouse and the small screen kicked into life.

After selecting the internet icon, he tapped the Puzzle Train website address on the once white, but now yellowing keyboard.

Tom stared at the screen as slowly the images revealed themselves and his excitement at completing the puzzles began to increase.

The mouse icon hovered expectantly over where Tom expected the link to be.

"Hey!" The screen in front of Tom went blank.

"Be quiet, young man," Mrs Stokes called over from her desk.

Tom looked over his shoulder at her, but all he saw was the large figure of Mr. Griffon looking down at him. Underneath a heavy frown were small eyes, a red nose and an evil grin.

"Your stepfather warned me that you might try and use the school computers. He asked me to make sure you get outside and get some fresh air."

"But, it's raining," protested Tom. "Anyway, I won't be very long."

"You won't be any time at all. Come on, out you go!" Mr. Griffon pulled the chair away from the desk.

"But Phil can't do that, it's not fair," a lump came to Tom's throat as he slowly headed for the library door.

"He's listed on your school form as your guardian, so yes he can." Mr. Griffon opened the door for Tom and waved him through. "Mrs Stokes, this boy is not allowed on the computers. Inform me immediately if he comes back in here."

"Definitely, Mr. Griffon. He's a disturbance to the other children anyway."

Tom's shoulders sagged as he was escorted from the library. There were less than six hours to go until the Puzzle Train applications closed. What was he going to do now?

Chapter 3 – Qualification puzzles

"That's totally unfair. Phil can't stop you going in the library." Isabelle's mind went quickly through all the people she could complain to. The list quickly escalated through the headmaster, the school governors, to the mayor and then a harshly worded letter to the President himself.

"He can, Issy. With Griffon around, he can," Tom muttered unhappily, as they walked down the street away from the school gates. "The competition closes at six tonight. I've barely got three hours left. What am I going to do?" He turned to stare at Isabelle, eyes wide, tears forming at the corners.

"Bring your laptop around to my house. You can use our Wi-Fi."

"Are you sure, Issy?" Tom swallowed hard.

"Yes, we spoke about how unfair Phil was being last night at dinner. Mom said I should tell you. Then you had the library idea so I didn't mention it."

"Thank you, Issy. And thank your mom for me. I'll see you soon." He couldn't contain himself and started running home.

Isabelle lived only a few blocks away, but when Tom arrived he was out of breath and sweating heavily. His laptop clutched in one hand, he knocked several times on the door with his other.

"In you come, Tom," said Isabelle's mom. "No need to pound the door down."

"Thank you, Mrs Edwards," said Tom.

"Tom, we've spoke about this, you can call me Sindy." She closed the door behind Tom. "I've spoken to Trudi, she'll come and fetch you later."

"Thank you," he started running up the stairs to Isabelle's room, where they connected his laptop to the Wi-Fi.

"I'll be downstairs in the study," called Isabelle as she opened her bedroom door. "Mom and I are going to do some research for a project."

Tom nodded and looked at his laptop. He entered the website address and drummed his fingers on the desk impatiently.

"Come on, come on, come on, come on!" Tom urged his computer to hurry up.

"Come on!" he said again beginning to get annoyed.

Unfortunately, his laptop didn't respond and continued at its own pace. Tom often found it would ignore him, especially when he was in a hurry. He wondered why Isabelle regularly called him impatient. If things worked quicker, Tom thought, he wouldn't need to be so impatient.

"Yes." He breathed a sigh of relief as finally the Puzzle Train logo appeared across the top of the screen.

At the top left was a picture of Marvin from the shoulders up, smiling as usual, wearing a very colorful bow tie with the numbers 498 on it.

498 Puzzle Train episodes so far.

At the top right was the familiar shape of the Conductor's silhouette sitting at his desk. On one side of the desk was the black outline of a computer screen and telephone on the desk. On the other, the silhouette of a toy steam train. Many times, Tom had studied that picture of the Conductor, but there was no way to make out any of his features. Who are you? he thought as he scrolled down.

Under this was an aerial picture of the train travelling through open countryside by the coast, the blue diesel engine with 'Puzzle Train' in gold lettering along its side. Behind it were the six beige carriages, each containing a puzzle, each numbered in purple, cutting through the greenery of the trees and grassy fields on the one side and the sea on the other. The waves were breaking against the cliff while a seagull hovered, almost as if it was watching the train go past. Tom loved that picture. He mentally placed himself inside the carriage solving one of the Conductor's most fiendish puzzles whilst he could smell the salty tang from the sea.

He scrolled down past the links to view highlights of the latest show and an invitation to subscribe to the newsletter, until he found what he was looking for. Halfway down the page on the right was the banner reading:

If you are between the ages of ten and twelve and would like to enter the competition to take part in the Puzzle Train, 'click here'. Entries close in...

02 HOURS 05 MINUTES 03 SECONDS

Just over two hours remaining! He watched the green digital timer tock down for a few seconds. He had cut it close.

Tom clicked 'here' and a registration page appeared. He entered his name, surname, date of birth, phone number and email address and clicked on the 'Submit' button.

A shadowy picture of the Conductor appeared on the screen, with the words 'please wait' showing on his desk. Tom noticed that the silhouette of the train had been replaced by a model roller coaster. He wondered why the Conductor kept changing the things on his desk.

"Who are you?" Tom said out loud to the picture of the Conductor. Tom was on his own so nobody replied.

Text appeared on the screen:

Welcome, Tom, puzzles we have plenty,
You will be allocated three out of twenty.
Complete them in the fastest time you can,
If qualification is your plan.
Then write well, for your sake,
One hundred words for the tie break.
The Conductor always has the final say.
But, what do you think he does all day?

Click 'here' to continue.

Tom read the poem and then clicked on the word 'Here'. Marvin's head and shoulders appeared on the screen. He was wearing a turquoise triangular party hat.

"Here comes your first puzzle. Good luck!"

A grid popped up, filling the left side of the screen, ten squares by ten. Each square contained what seemed to be a random letter. On the top right of the screen appeared a digital clock showing two minutes. Underneath the clock in large font, fourteen words appeared, all associated with trains and the show. There were no other clues and the clock started to count down.

"A word search," Tom beamed.

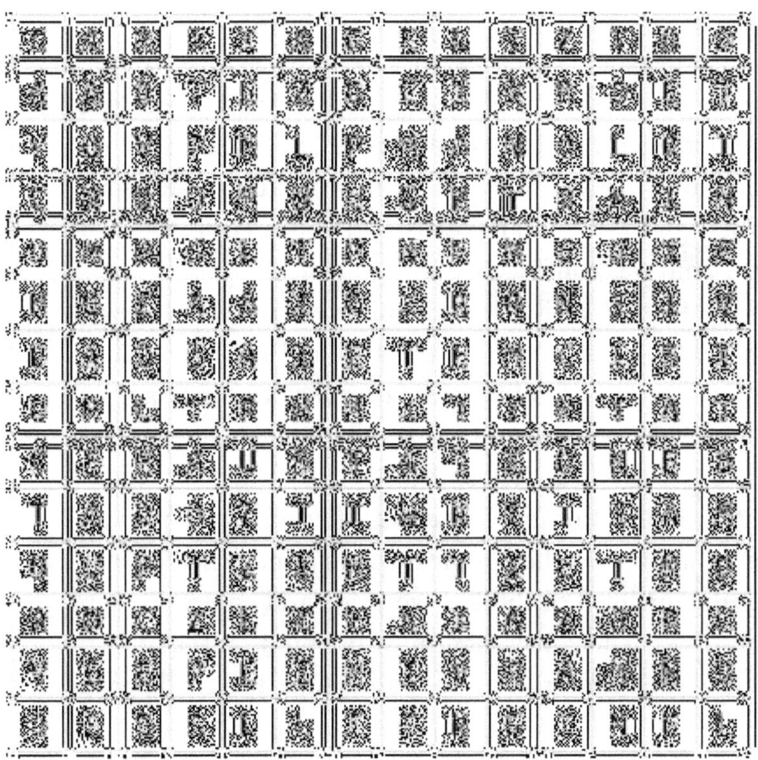

Tom looked at the grid for a few seconds then moved the mouse onto it and highlighted STATION. The word 'Station' disappeared from the list. He quickly found the remaining words with twenty-seven seconds left on the clock. He leant back on the chair feeling very pleased with himself.

Marvin reappeared. The turquoise triangular party hat was now adorned with a silver bow. "Congratulations, you have completed your first puzzle. Here comes puzzle number two."

"Thanks, Marvin," Tom said to his laptop. Marvin, unsurprisingly didn't answer. In Tom's head though Marvin was asking him what he would spend the money on when he won.

The screen went grey and then another ten-by-ten grid appeared filling the left-hand half of the screen. Surely not another word search, thought Tom. But then an identical ten-by-ten grid showed to the right of it and an equals sign appeared in between the two grids. Tom was confused.

Three squares on the left grid suddenly went red. They stayed there for only a few seconds before the grid and the red squares disappeared, replaced by a familiar green digital clock, showing just fifteen seconds. The clock started ticking down immediately.

"Huh!" Tom frowned at the blank grid.

Thoughts spiralled through his mind. After all those episodes he had watched and re-watched of the Puzzle Train, he had an idea how the Conductor liked to think. Two grids and an equals sign were the only clues. The equals sign must be important. Left grid equals right grid. The two grids must be the same. Then it dawned on him.

"Match the squares!"

Here are three of Tom's grids. On the next page are blank grids. Can you memorise the location of the colored squares and replicate on the grids on the next page?

Grid 1

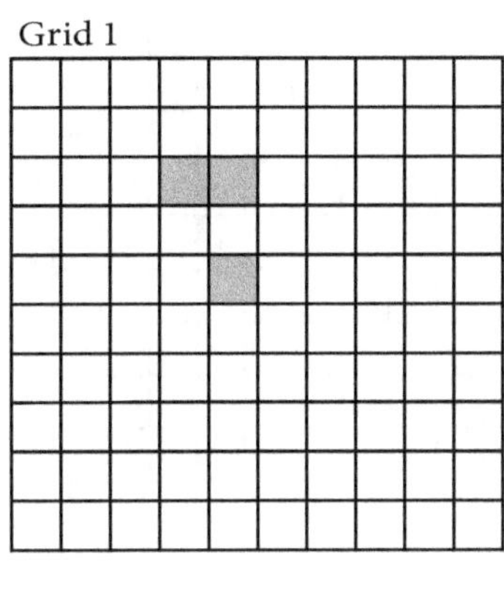

Grid 2

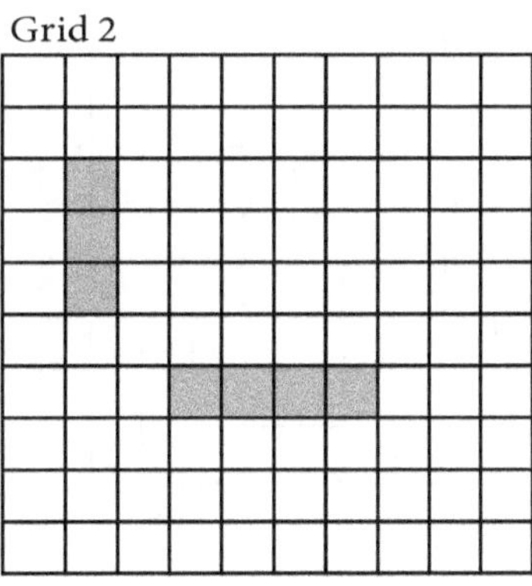

Grid 3

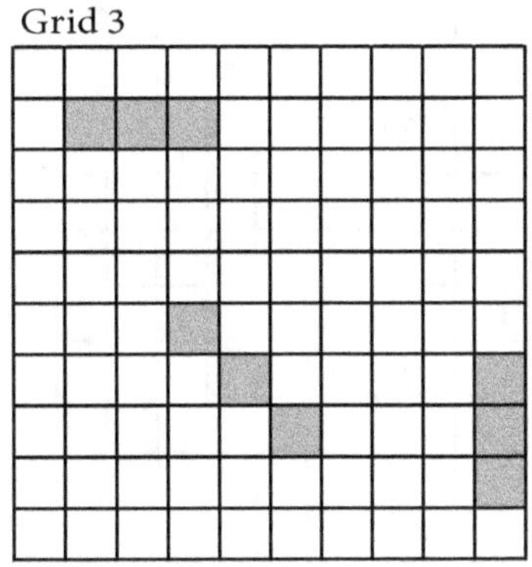

Can you complete the grids below to match the shading of the grids on the previous page?

Grid 1

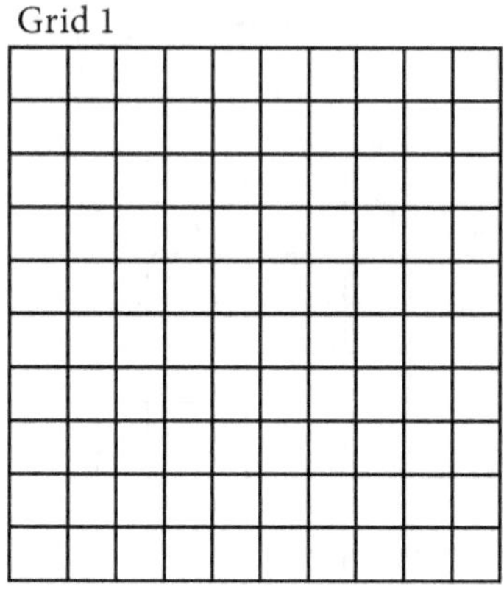

Grid 2

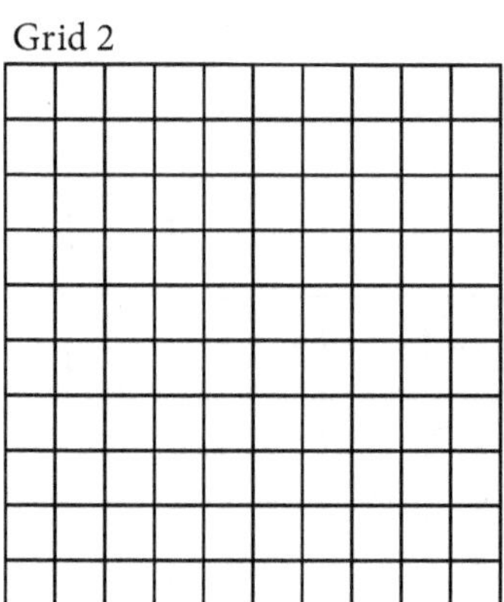

Grid 3

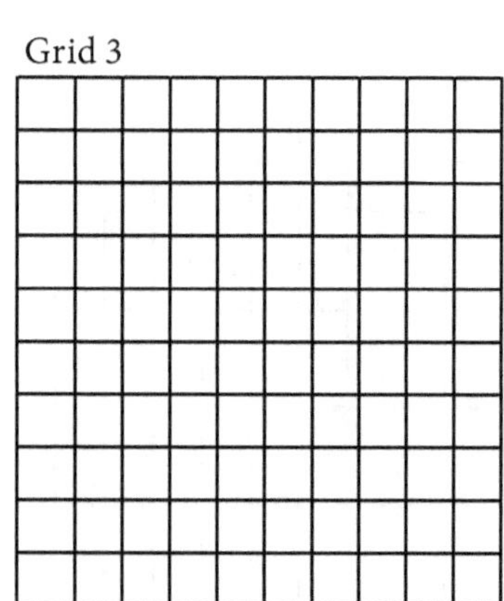

He hovered the mouse over where he thought the squares were and held his breath. Was this right? He had seen where the squares were but he hadn't taken much notice. He closed his eyes and tried to picture the position of the red squares as they had appeared in the right-hand grid. He was aware of the clock counting down. Six seconds! No time to hesitate now. He clicked the first square. It turned red. Then he clicked on the next two in quick succession.

"Correct," appeared on the screen. "Four to go," appeared underneath.

Tom exhaled and resolved to concentrate harder.

The number of squares increased with each new grid and the patterns became more complicated. Next was four squares, then six, then nine.

He completed them easily. The final pattern consisted of twelve squares placed at random. The grid disappeared, Tom clicked where he thought the red squares were.

"Where was that last one?" he wailed at his laptop. He couldn't remember. Three seconds, two, one.

Panic. Click. He selected where he thought the final square was.

'**ERROR!**' flashed on the screen.

"Bah!" Tom made a hand gesture at his screen. Marvin's face appeared looking very sad.

"Last chance," said Marvin.

The final puzzle repeated itself; this time Tom concentrated and entered the correct combination. Marvin re-appeared, wearing his hat, the bow and a silver headband with the words '**WELL DONE!**' in green writing on it.

"Congratulations and now it's time to move on to the third and final puzzle," announced Marvin.

Text appeared on the screen:

This is your last puzzle, don't neglect it,
In Marvin's house everything is where you expect it.
At 9:02 he wearily arrives home,
Parks in the drive all alone.
2 minutes it takes to hang coat and hat,
Turns the TV on 14 minutes after that,
An hour and 20 later he washes his face and hands,
78 minutes before that, he stands,
Looking out the window at flowers so dry,
5 minutes to water and then with a sigh.
60 seconds to put the car to bed,
Hang the keys up then he scratches his head,
With clean hands his hunger he has to fix,
But where was he at 9:26?

Choose one:
Kitchen
Bedroom
Bathroom
Living room
Garden
Attic
Garage
Cellar
Hallway
Driveway
You have five minutes to answer. You only have one chance.

The Conductor's love of poems was familiar to anyone who watched the Puzzle Train. And Tom watched more than most. The clues at the beginning of each carriage were always a poem. The puzzleteers were given a minute to think about the clue. Tom would always try to crack the clue with them.

Tom scanned down the lines quickly, muttering as he went.

"Everything's where we expect it to be. 9:04 he must be in the hallway. TV at … 9:18. Then … 9:20. Looking out the window. Where is he then? Ok, keep going. 9:25 he finishes watering the flowers then … 9:26! That's it. He's with the car."

He moved the mouse over the 'Driveway' but something made him stop.

"Put the car to bed. What does that mean? Wait, he put it away for the night, he must have put it in his garage!"

He clicked 'garage' and sat back in the chair.

Marvin's head and shoulders appeared once more. The triangular party hat was replaced by a very grand looking white top hat which had the words 'Puzzle Champion' written in red.

"Yes!" Tom jumped up from the chair, arms aloft.

"Congratulations. You have passed three puzzle challenges. Now in one hundred words or less you must describe what you think the Conductor does in a day. You have five minutes!"

Marvin disappeared and a box for Tom to type the answer appeared in the centre of the screen with these words already typed in it.

I think that the Conductor spends his day...

At the same time the green digital clock appeared set at five minutes. It started ticking down and Tom stared at the screen. He sat quickly, hands hovering over the keyboard waiting for the words to come, but they didn't. His mind went totally blank. What *would* the Conductor do all day?

Why hadn't he asked Isabelle what she had written? She was so creative. She'd probably thought of something good. Why hadn't he thought about this during the day? He'd known this question would come up. He could have spent the day planning an amazing answer. He had been too busy daydreaming about being on the train and solving the puzzles. Tom was annoyed with himself and Phil's words went through his head.

'You just never focus on anything. Your mind is all over the place. You'll never amount to much. Sport will give you discipline. You're just lazy.'

Should I go downstairs and find her? The thought flashed through his mind. It would waste too much time, he decided. While Tom was busy getting annoyed with himself, the clock was busy ticking down.

Time remaining 03:56.

What would the Conductor do? Tom had never thought about it. He was fixated with who the Conductor was and what he looked like, not what he did.

Tom's mind finally started working, but rather than being focussed, it was wandering. He knew the Conductor spent a lot of time sitting behind his desk. He's probably designing puzzles. He supposed he had to get up some time and go to the bathroom at the very least. And maybe he would make a cup of tea as well. Did he watch TV? Shout at Marvin? Tom didn't think any of these things sounded very interesting.

He racked his brain trying to think of something.

Time remaining 03:05.

Keep calm, use your instincts, take a deep breath, hold it and count to ten. Then do whatever you were going to do. That was a much more pleasant voice in Tom's head. It belonged to his gran.

As instructed, Tom took a deep breath, held it and counted to ten. His head cleared and he just started typing.

"...on trains. He lives, eats and sleeps on a train. One carriage is his bedroom, one is his living room. There's one carriage where he has his desk and creates all his puzzles. And there is one which just contains a massive train set. The Conductor was sent by a highly intelligent alien species to test mankind to see whether we are ready to be given the gift of interstellar travel. Their spaceships look like earth trains. In the afternoons Marvin brings him an ice cream with caramel sauce, for relaxation."

The word count at the bottom of the text box showed ninety-one words. That's not too bad thought Tom. Then the time ran out. Tom had no idea where the vision of Marvin bringing the Conductor ice cream came from. Maybe it was because he fancied an ice cream now, and caramel sauce was his favorite.

Marvin's face reappeared. This time there was no hat, just a white bow tie with 'thank you' written on it in red.

"Your application has been successfully sent. Winners will be announced on Friday from 4pm." His face disappeared and Tom was taken back to the main website.

Tom heaved a sigh of relief. It was done, and he would find out tomorrow whether his application would be accepted.

Tom browsed the website for a while, until he heard his mom arrive to collect him. They chatted as Trudi drove the short distance home.

"Normally I wouldn't consider going behind Phil's back like that, but he's been totally unreasonable ever since he started his new job."

"Since before then," Tom snorted.

"He just wants you to try harder at school. And I agree with him, it wouldn't hurt you to improve your grades." The car spluttered as they came to a halt at a stop street. Tom slouched down, just in case he saw anyone he knew.

The car took off in a puff of smoke with a whine from the engine.

"And he hates the Puzzle Train. He's always telling me it's trash and I should be playing outside," said Tom.

"Nothing would make me happier than to see you take part on the train." Trudi gave Tom's knee a squeeze. "Just make sure you do your homework when you get home."

A grateful Tom went upstairs and started his homework. He quickly got stuck and sent Isabelle a message asking her what the answer was.

A few minutes later, a message came through that made Tom smile. "Check page 74 of the text book. That will help."

"Thanks, Issy," Tom replied. Then he thought for a moment and typed out a second message.

"Hey, Issy, how amazing would it be if we were on the Puzzle Train together?"

Chapter 4 – A Long Friday

Friday morning and school was bustling as it always was before the first lesson. Talk was only about the Puzzle Train. It seemed as if every eligible child in the school had entered. And even some that weren't eligible. Two main themes quickly developed:

"How would you spend your five million dollars?" and "How cool would it be to be a national TV star?"

The bell rang and it seemed as if the school gave a collective groan. Tom moped off to his first class of the day, English.

"Open your text books at page forty-two. And we'll have no talk of the Puzzle Train, thank you very much." Mrs Henderson was not a teacher to be taken lightly. A large lady with a quick temper who was quick to dish out a detention or four.

Tom tried to pay attention for a few minutes and then his mind drifted to the Puzzle Train and his application. Had he really written the Conductor was sent by aliens? Why had he put that? What was he thinking?

The bell rang for the end of the lesson. He left the classroom and walked outside into a cool breeze and a fine drizzle. Hunched over with his hands in his pockets he made his way to the tree to meet Isabelle.

"What's up with you?" Isabelle asked. "I thought you'd be excited about the results later?"

"I'm not happy with my answer about the Conductor. I think it's stupid!" He kicked the tree in frustration. It didn't make him feel better.

A cool breeze came across the playing field and the drizzle became a little heavier.

"That sounds like your stepfather talking! You can't write anything stupid because no one knows what he does. That's why it was such a brilliant question."

"I should have asked you what you wrote."

"You could have. But you didn't. Maybe I wouldn't have told you anyway," Isabelle teased. "Besides, you had two days to think about what to write."

"I did think that last night as I was struggling to think of something. And then that five-minute timer started ticking down and my mind went blank." Tom was waving his arms around to emphasise his frustration.

"So, what did you write?"

"All about the Conductor being an alien." Tom was going red with embarrassment as he said the words.

"Huh?" Isabelle concealed a smile. "An alien?"

As Tom spoke he could feel his chances of ever being selected fade away.

"I said he's really an alien and he has been sent to test humankind."

Isabelle started laughing. "You never did!"

"Yup." Tom could feel a lump in the back of his throat and his voice was very small and squeaky. He fought back a tear.

"Why are you getting upset now, Tom?"

"You would be upset too if you had written about how the Conductor is an alien. Oh, and an alien who likes ice cream too!"

"Well, ice cream is normal enough at least. I'm sure that will be far from the weirdest application. Maybe I said the Conductor is, umm, a giraffe in disguise."

"Why would you do that?"

"Well that's the point isn't it? I mean, no one knows how the Conductor spends his day. It would have to be a pretty darn good disguise."

"Come on, tell me. What did you write?"

The bell rang. Time to get back to lessons.

"Sorry, Tom, got to go. See you at lunch." Isabelle skipped off towards her classroom.

Tom put his hands in his pockets and his head down and turned towards his own classroom.

What did she write? Why didn't I ask her yesterday?

Tom's thoughts continued as he walked to his classroom. She's such a goody-goody, he thought. Who would want to hurry to lessons? The drizzle became a little heavier and was becoming more like rain. Cold water began to soak through his top and shirt and he could feel water seeping in through his shoes as he walked through the wet grass. Maybe running wasn't such a bad idea after all. He quickened his pace and started to run.

All anyone could talk about at school was the Puzzle Train. Chatter about the Puzzle Train continued as the minutes passed by and the announcement became closer. Even the weather seemed excited as the grey clouds parted to allow some sun through.

"What did you say the Conductor does all day?" Tom asked Isabelle as soon as he saw her under their tree at lunch time.

"Okay then, I suppose I'll tell you," Isabelle conceded. "I said the Conductor doesn't really exist. He's a computer-generated figment of Marvin's imagination. Marvin changes his voice by computer and pretends to be really mean."

Tom looked shocked. "Do you think that's true?"

"I don't know, but I thought it was funny. Can you really imagine Marvin being mean? He always seems so happy."

"Yes, I s'pose so." Tom screwed up his face.

They spent the rest of lunch time discussing how amazing it would be to appear on the Puzzle Train. On the way back to class Tom was thinking about the Conductor being computer generated. It couldn't be true. Could it? But then maybe Isabelle could be right. She was the cleverest person Tom knew and, after all, no one had ever seen his face or knew who he was. Tom couldn't decide whether he thought the Conductor was real or not. He had been desperate to find out who the Conductor was, but now he was beginning to think he might not even exist.

"What if you're right, Issy?" He looked at her as they walked towards class. "It's all a waste of time, watching the show, the highlights, the blogs, the online chats. If he doesn't exist then it's all pointless."

"In the eight years I've known you, I've never heard you talk like this Tom. All those times you've talked to me about him. And there have been a lot. I mean loads."

"You make it sound like I talk about nothing else."

Isabelle gave Tom a long look but decided not to respond.

"He has to exist, Tom. They couldn't have a show based on a lie like that."

"Yeah, I suppose you're right," Tom shrugged. His voice was quiet and he was looking at his shoes.

"If any team did ever win, I'm sure he would be there waiting for them!" Isabelle was upbeat.

Tom glanced up at her, an unhappy look on his face.

"Are you really telling me that now, if you won a spot on the show, you wouldn't go?" Isabelle asked.

"Maybe."

"Wouldn't you still want to go on the train?"

"I suppose so," Tom conceded.

"And meet Marvin?"

"Well, yes, I guess." Tom started smiling.

"And attempt the puzzles?"

"Yes, I would love to attempt the puzzles, more than anything!" Tom's grin was now wide.

"Great," said Isabelle. "That's the Tom I know."

"Just Mr. Griffon's history lesson to go and then the winners are announced this evening!" Tom felt ten feet tall as they entered the school building.

Tom rapidly deflated six feet within minutes of Mr. Griffon's history lesson. Despite all his best efforts to listen and learn, Tom quickly found himself daydreaming about being on the Puzzle Train. He was there in carriage six with Isabelle, looking for the right key.

"Pay attention!" snapped a voice in the distance.

"Nearly there." Tom was imagining he was carefully placing the key in the lock.

"Tom, pay attention!" the voice was louder this time, closer.

Tom was rudely denied a place in Puzzle Train folklore by a podgy hand being slapped on his desk.

"Were you daydreaming, Tom?" asked Mr. Griffon with a deep frown across his face. Wrinkles seemed to run all the way up his bald head.

"No, Mr. Griffon. Sorry."

"Pay attention, Tom. How many times do I have to tell you?" the teacher shouted.

Tom went red. There was something about Mr. Griffon he didn't like. He looked across to the desk next to him and opened his text book to the correct page. It would at least look as if he was paying attention. Then his thoughts drifted back to the Puzzle Train.

Had they already decided who will go on the show? What puzzles had the Conductor planned? What would the other five children be like? How many children had applied? Millions? He imagined himself talking to Marvin.

"Tom."

He imagined himself in carriage one looking at the first puzzle.

"Tom!"

He imagined himself asking the Conductor for his prizes.

"TOM TREADWELL. For the last time, pay attention!" Tom's legacy as a legend of the Puzzle Train was ruined for the second time in quick succession. Had anyone ever lost the Puzzle Train twice in one history lesson? Tom doubted it.

"What did I just ask you?" Mr. Griffon was close enough that Tom could smell his bad breath and see the creases in his ugly brown suit.

"Umm." Tom hadn't heard a word Mr. Griffon had been saying. What were we studying, he wondered? He looked at his open text book but it didn't offer any help.

"UMM!" Mr. Griffon shouted back at him. "Is 'umm' all you can say?" Even his bald head seemed to turn red with anger. Tom thought that any moment steam would come out of his ears.

"I shall be sending an email home to your parents, for the second time this week!" he continued before Tom could even answer.

Any excuse to email Phil, Tom thought. Griffon always contacted Phil rather than his mom. There would definitely be an argument. But it didn't matter because that night the winners would be announced, the six lucky children. It could be him, Tom thought. He could be on the Puzzle Train!

Tom and Isabelle talked of nothing else except the Puzzle Train as they walked home after school.

They reached Isabelle's house first and bade each other "Good luck!" and Tom headed for home, wondering why Mr. Griffon was so angry. And what was he talking about anyway? Had any teacher ever been as angry at a student for not paying attention in class?

Neither car was home, so Tom let himself in, turned the Wi-Fi on and rushed upstairs, hoping that Phil had reset the password.

"Wow," he told his laptop as it connected straight away. "Phil's switched the Wi-Fi password back now the qualification puzzles are over. He really doesn't want me to take part in the Puzzle Train." His laptop said nothing back.

He typed in the Puzzle Train website address and sat back as the images downloaded in front of him.

Chapter 5 - Announcements

There, on the website, was the familiar digital clock with its green display, counting down and showing twenty-three minutes. Above it a banner spread across the screen:

The first lucky winner
to appear on the children's episode
of

The Puzzle Train

will be announced in:
00 HOURS 23 MINUTES 16 SECONDS

The clock counted down, second by slow second.

Tom tried to keep himself busy for the next twenty-three minutes but it wasn't easy. He looked at his school books, in a pile on his bedroom floor, and thought about doing his homework. The thought didn't last long though. Instead he logged on to his video game and started playing, but he found it difficult to concentrate.

Twenty-two minutes dragged by and Tom switched from his game to the Puzzle Train website. The clock was showing forty-seven seconds to go. Tom watched the countdown on the screen. Had time ever passed so slowly? Maybe only in Mr. Griffon's Friday afternoon history class.

Finally, the clock showed zero and was replaced with Marvin.

"Good evening, everybody. I have some fantastic news for one lucky entrant for the children's edition of the Puzzle Train. Let me delay no further, the first lucky winner is…" Marvin made the word 'is' last for several seconds, getting louder until he stopped and paused for effect. He took a deep breath and said,

"Shaun Hegerty!" He applauded.

"Congratulations, Shaun. Confirmation and full details will be sent to you by email in the next few minutes, so don't go anywhere."

Tom voiced his disappointment long and loud at his laptop. If the computer could have spoken, it would have told him to be quiet and wait a half hour. It couldn't so it didn't.

Instead, the voice coming through its speakers belonged to Marvin. "Our next lucky winner will be announced in thirty minutes."

The digital clock reappeared.

Tom could just hear Phil in his head.

"The Puzzle Train is a waste of time. Why don't you take up a sport or a hobby?"

Tom wished Phil would take up more sport. Mountain climbing or round the world yachting sprung to mind.

Tom tried to wait patiently but he found it very hard, so he waited impatiently instead.

As before when the time ticked down to zero, Marvin appeared on the screen.

"Welcome back, everyone. I'm sure you are all eager to hear who our next young puzzleteer will be. And I am delighted to be able to tell you, our second lucky winner is…." Once again Marvin extended the word 'is' to build the tension. There was a long pause again.

"Come on!" yelled Tom.

"Is-a-belle Ed-wards!"

"Congratulations, Isabelle! An email is being typed to you at this very moment. Don't go anywhere, our third winner will be announced in thirty minutes."

"Grr!" Tom snarled at his laptop. But then it dawned on him. That name sounded familiar.

Isabelle!

Isabelle would be appearing on the Puzzle Train! This was huge. He grabbed his phone and started to type:

"Hey, Issy, wow, AWESOME!"

"I can't believe it!" Isabelle replied at once.

"So cool!"

"Can't wait!" came her reply with at least a hundred smiley faces.

Tom was really pleased for Isabelle but at the same time he was jealous. He wanted to go on the Puzzle Train more than he had ever wanted anything before and now there were only four spots remaining.

To pass the next thirty minutes he imagined watching Isabelle on TV in the Puzzle Train. He knew she would be great and he couldn't help being happy for her.

Thirty minutes dragged past and Marvin announced that Holly Grayson was the third lucky winner. Tom was beginning to feel despondent now. Half the places were filled and there were still thousands, maybe millions, of other children who could be chosen to go on the train with Isabelle.

If he asked her nicely, maybe he could come to the station with her. Even to see the train in real life would be awesome. Maybe he could even get a selfie with Marvin, or a glimpse of the Conductor. Would that be too much to hope for?

Another thirty minutes passed and Marvin was back on the screen looking happy. Tom did not feel happy, especially when he announced that the fourth lucky winner was Harvey Roberts. Only two places left now, Tom thought.

Time continued to pass slowly. The thirty minutes before Marvin announced the fifth lucky winner seemed like hours. He looked around his bedroom at everything, tried to read a book, and play his video game. He even paced around the house, but nothing seemed to help the time pass by any quicker.

With nothing else holding his attention, he watched the last three minutes tick down, second by agonising second, with longing, hope, desperation and impatience in equal measure.

Marvin reappeared on the screen when the timer clicked to zero, looking as happy as Tom could ever remember seeing him. "Our fifth lucky puzzleteer to take part in the children's episode is…." The now familiar extending of 'is' and the pause seemed longer than before. Tom crossed his fingers and shut his eyes, praying his name would be announced.

"George Irveine!

Congratulations, George! We look forward to welcoming you on board. Our sixth and final puzzleteer will be announced in thirty minutes."

"N-o-o-o-o!" exclaimed Tom as he opened his eyes to see Marvin being replaced by the green digital clock.

He stamped his feet, picked up his homework book and threw it on the bed in frustration. He didn't hear his mom arrive and come in through the front door.

"Hey, what's going on up there?"

"Nothing," Tom called down sulkily.

"Well make sure 'nothing' happens more quietly next time."

"Will do, Mom."

Tom started his video game, then checked his phone. There was a message from Isabelle.

"Researcher is here."

"What for?"

"From PT. Checking with my parents that it's OK for me to go on the show!"

"Wow, that was quick!"

One chance left, millions of other children. Tom could feel the desperation in his stomach. Twenty-eight and a half minutes still to go. Tom put his phone in his pocket and returned to his video game. Lucky Isabelle, he thought. After what seemed to be hours, he checked the website once again. There were only three minutes left. And then the butterflies came back. This was it. His final chance.

He heard an engine and peered out the window. His heart sank when he saw Phil pull up outside the house and get out of his car, slamming the door behind him. The front door opened with a crash.

"Twice in one week!" Phil shouted as he walked in the house.

"I don't believe it. Where is he?" He was furious.

"What is it, Phil?" Tom's mom came from the kitchen.

"Not paying attention in Mr. Griffon's history class!"

He showed the email on his phone to Trudi.

"AGAIN!" he shouted.

"Tom, get down here, please," his mom called up the stairs.

"NOW!" added Phil stamping on the hall floor. Tom looked at the digital clock counting down, just over two and a half minutes to go. There was no getting out of this. Phil was seriously angry so he reluctantly walked down the stairs.

"Dining room!" Phil barked the order out. Tom had no choice but to follow him slowly down the hall and into the dining room.

Phil and his mom sat on one side of the table, Tom sat on the other. He felt small and silly. He swallowed nervously and prepared himself for what was to come.

"What is the meaning of this?" Phil said angrily and held the phone for Tom to see the email from Mr. Griffon. "Not paying attention in class, again!" he continued without giving Tom any time to answer.

"Tom, we're very disappointed," added his mom. "You said you would make more of an effort this term."

Tom swallowed hard. "Yeah, but I don't like history, and besides it's the announcement of the winners for the Puzzle Train tonight so I was thinking about that." His eyes shifted from his mom to Phil to the table. He instantly realised that mentioning the

Puzzle Train was a bad move. "Mr. Griffon picks on me. I'm not the only one not paying attention."

"The Puzzle Train is a total waste of time. Get that in your head! You need to knuckle down and work hard at school!" Phil shouted.

Tom could feel a lump in his throat and fought back the tears he could feel starting in his eyes as Phil shouted at him.

"You're grounded for the rest of the month and next month! You'll have plenty of time to think about your stupid Puzzle Train then!" Phil pointed at him. He was shaking with rage and his face was beginning to turn red.

"And no laptop. That's coming with me to the office!"

Tom's bottom lip was quivering now.

"No, I'm sorry. Please don't take my laptop!" Tom begged. Phil's grin was malicious. He had found Tom's weak spot.

His phone buzzed in his pocket. Probably Isabelle telling me how awesome everything was with the researcher. The thought made him feel worse.

Then it buzzed again and again and again until his leg was beginning to get numb. He took it out and saw he had twenty-seven messages. He put it on the dining table where it continued to buzz loudly on the wooden surface. Thirty-nine messages.

"What's going on?" His mom picked up the phone quickly before Tom could react. She read some of the messages. "It seems your friends are congratulating you on being the sixth child to be selected for the Puzzle Train."

"What? I can't believe it. It must be a joke," said Tom unhappily. The lump in his throat seemed to be growing larger.

"Give me that!" Phil snatched the phone from Trudi and started reading the messages.

"Hey, that's private," complained Tom. "Give it back!"

The malicious grin grew larger on Phil's pointy face and his eyes went as wide as saucers.

"It's right, you have been selected to go on the Puzzle Train. Look!" There was an official email on the small screen from the Puzzle Train. Phil showed it to Tom.

Tom's heart leapt, the lump in his throat disappeared, the tears in his eyes were now tears of joy. This was the best moment of his entire life ever. He wanted to jump up and down, shout and scream at the top of his voice that he would be on the Puzzle Train. He kept calm on the outside knowing how much it would irritate Phil, but his insides were performing back flips with excitement.

"There's one problem." Phil's voice was calm and quiet but had an evil undertone to it.

"W-w-what?" said Tom quietly.

"You're grounded." The malicious grin on his face grew and stretched from one of Phil's pointy ears to the other. "And you're not going to go!"

"Now hang on, Phil!" Trudi turned to stare at him.

"What… you can't… that's not fair." Tom cut across her, the lump in his throat came back. Tears started to well up in his eyes. He was crushed.

Phil leaned over the dining table, his face getting ever closer to Tom's.

"Oh, I can and I will. They need permission for you to go and I'm not going to give it," he said quietly and menacingly.

Tom got up from the chair and ran down the hall and up the stairs to his bedroom. He slammed the door, flung himself on his bed and couldn't stop the stream of tears as he wailed and sobbed into his pillow.

Chapter 6 – Lester Vince

Tom wasn't sure how long he cried for but he eventually stopped and looked around surprised at how dark his room had become. His eyes were red and sore and his nose was full of snot. He went to the bathroom and blew hard on a piece of toilet paper. On his way back, he heard an argument coming from the dining room downstairs. Voices were raised and tempers short. They were arguing about the Puzzle Train. Tom sat on the top of the stairs and tried to listen.

The doorbell rang. Its happy chime felt out of place with Tom's mood and the atmosphere in the house.

"Well, I'm going to answer it anyway," his mom shouted defiantly to Phil. Tom heard her soft footsteps as she walked down the hall.

"Good evening, Mrs Treadwell. My name is Lester Vince." Lester was calm and polite. Totally contrary to the argument that had been raging only seconds before.

"Umm, now's not really a good time." Trudi glanced at the man wearing a brown suit and carrying a battered briefcase. "We don't buy on the doorstep."

"Ah, but I'm not selling anything. I have been sent by the Puzzle Train. May I come in? Your son has been selected to appear. I'm sure you have heard?"

Tom heard Phil's footsteps stomping down the hall.

"Well you can just leave because he's not going on the show. He's grounded!" Phil snapped at Lester.

Tom crawled as quietly as he could down the first two stairs, so he could see what was happening at the front door. He propped himself up on his hands two more stairs down and could just see through the railing.

Lester was not at all disturbed by Phil's rudeness.

"Good evening, sir, you must be Tom's father. You must be so proud." He held out his hand for Phil to shake.

"I'm his stepfather and he's not going. He's grounded," Phil said. The harshness in his voice was still there and he ignored Lester's hand. He began to shut the front door in his face when Tom's mom pushed him out of the way.

"I do apologise for Phil. Please do come in."

Lester stepped inside closing the front door behind him and followed Trudi.

"It's in a mess," she said apologetically as she hastily pulled the living room door shut. "We weren't expecting visitors. Come through to the dining room." She led the way. Phil reluctantly followed.

Tom crept down three or four further steps so he could better hear what was going on.

There was a scrape of chairs as the three of them made themselves comfortable around the dining table. Trudi offered tea which Lester declined.

"The Conductor has sent me personally to meet with you to ensure that everything is in order and Tom has parental permission to come on the Puzzle Train. And, of course, that he is between the ages of ten and twelve."

"Well, he can't go! He's been slacking off at school again and he's grounded," Phil said for the third time.

"There's no way he's going to miss out on this opportunity just because he wasn't paying attention in class! We've discussed this."

Tom's heart leapt every time his mom defended him. He was surprised to hear just how firm her voice was.

"Yes, this would be the opportunity of a lifetime for anyone," Lester said. "Places on the Puzzle Train are highly sought after. We have a waiting list of nearly three years for the adult version." There was a hint of pride in his voice.

"I don't care. He needs to work harder at school. This will teach him a lesson!" Phil sat back with his arms folded.

"I think incentive is greater than punishment. I'm sure Tom's grades will improve after this opportunity. I must say, according to our statistics, Tom completed the puzzles quicker than almost everyone. He's a remarkably bright boy."

"I don't care what you think. It's a shame he doesn't show any of that brightness in his school grades."

"Different people find interest in all kinds of different things." Lester reached into his briefcase and retrieved a form.

"He will hate you forever if you don't let him go, Phil, and I want you two to get on," Trudi said, putting her hand on his shoulder.

Phil was silent for a moment. A secret debate raging behind his eyes.

"No." He sat back on the chair and folded his arms. "He can't go."

"Phil!" Tom's mom glared at him. "How could you? It will crush him."

"Actually, if I may interject …" Lester pushed the form across the table. "Did you say you were the boy's stepfather?"

"Well, we're not married," said Trudi. "But I like Tom to call Phil his stepfather."

"Well then, I only need your signature, Mrs Treadwell, as Tom's only legal guardian."

"It's Ms Treadwell. And I will sign, thank you." Even from on the stairs, Tom could hear the relief in her voice. Tom could have danced on the stairs with joy.

"All right, fine! He can go. But I'm not happy about it!" Phil sensed defeat and decided he would at least try and be gracious about it.

"That's fabulous," Lester said happily. "There's a contract here to sign as well, if you'd be so kind." He reached back into his briefcase and retrieved the document and a pen and slid them across the table.

"And I'd love to meet Tom if he's here," Lester continued.

"He's in his room." Trudi grabbed the pen and started completing the forms. "TOM," she called.

Tom came running down the stairs, along the hallway and into the dining room.

"Hello, young Tom," Lester said and held his hand out for Tom to shake, which he did enthusiastically.

"It's great to meet you. Congratulations for winning your place on the Puzzle Train. I just want to chat to you to find out a little about you for the show." He paused as Tom sat on one of the spare dining room chairs, trying to avoid Phil's glare. "Now, Tom, why did you apply to come on the show?"

"I love the Puzzle Train. It's my favorite show ever! It would be so cool to meet the Conductor. He's a genius!"

Phil scoffed and looked out the window.

"And what about school?" continued Lester.

"School's all right. Some of the time, anyway. Sometimes it's boring."

"You need to pay attention! Stop daydreaming," Phil interrupted moodily. "He's lazy and is always getting into trouble."

His mom looked up from completing the form and gave Phil a hard look.

"Well, it's true. All he does is watch TV and go on the internet. He needs a hobby, take up a sport, like golf."

"I don't like sport. I like puzzles." Tom stared at Phil.

"So, Tom, how often do you watch the show?" Lester continued.

"I never miss it. I watch every episode." Tom sat up straight and puffed out his chest. "And I watch the highlights on the website and YouTube."

"You see, obsessed." Phil shook his head. "Needs to get some fresh air."

"Phil, leave him," Tom's mom said. "That's enough for one evening!"

"He needs to improve his grades," Phil huffed.

"You'd better work harder at school now, Tom." His mom looked at him with a stern look on her face.

"Definitely!" Tom nodded vigorously. He thought of how his mom had stuck up for him in the argument with Phil. "Will you come with me to the station, mom?"

"We do need one parent to accompany each child," said Lester. "And filming will be tomorrow."

"Tomorrow!" Toms eyes were wide with shock.

"I'd love to," his mom told Lester. "Phil's got golf tomorrow, so it was just going to be Tom and I here anyway."

Phil ignored her comment. "It's all rather quick, isn't it? Announcing the winner one day and filming the next?"

"We felt it best," Lester explained. "We didn't think it would be right to have the children waiting for ages before filming. Plus, can you imagine all the fuss at school if tomorrow was a school day? We decided not to announce the filming day publicly either, please keep it confidential."

Tom thought about it. All his and Isabelle's friends would be asking them questions, wanting Marvin's autograph and selfies. He agreed with Lester. It would be a nightmare.

"What if we weren't at home?" scowled Phil.

"We have Tom's phone number and email address. We were confident we could get hold of him. And if not, we have a backup list of children we could contact."

Lester was making notes of the conversation as they talked.

"How did you get here so quickly?" said Tom excitedly.

"The Conductor had picked the winners in advance. There are researchers waiting by all the winners' houses."

"Did you go and see Isabelle first?" Tom said.

"Yes, I did. The Conductor was impressed with her, as he was with you! Do you know her?"

"She's my best friend. She's brilliant!" said Tom. "Have you met him, the Conductor I mean? What's he like?" The words blurted from his mouth. He couldn't suppress his excitement.

Lester chuckled. "Sorry, Tom, I just get an email from him."

Tom's mom finished filling in the form, signed it and handed it back to Lester who popped it into his briefcase.

"Thank you very much for your time. Tom, good luck on the show. A car will be here to pick you and your mom up at ten o'clock sharp tomorrow morning. Don't be late, the Conductor demands everything runs to time." He handed Tom a business card. "This has an access code on it. You can use this to log onto the website and check the car's details and whereabouts."

Trudi and Phil walked Lester to the front door where they shook hands. Even Phil did so this time.

"Thank you for coming," Trudi said as Lester walked down the drive towards his car. Phil just grunted.

Tom grabbed his phone off the dining table and went into the hall, every nerve jangling. Phil pointed at him from the front door and growled, "Consider yourself very, very lucky!"

Tom ran past Phil and up the stairs. He didn't want to be around his stepfather.

He jumped on his bed and started going through his text messages. Almost everyone in his school had sent him a congratulatory message. He ignored them and found the ones from Isabelle.

"What's going on? Where are you?" was the last one he received.

"Sorry, Issy, things mad here. Explain later. So excited!"

They messaged back and forth for a while until Isabelle said, "What will we do if one of us gets locked away?"

"We'll try not to get locked away in the first place," replied Tom.

"But what if one of us does?"

"Go ahead without me. I would love it if you could complete the puzzles. If I'm not there then at least I can watch you on TV afterwards."

"If I get locked in then the same applies."

"It's a deal."

"Deal."

After a while Tom's mom came into his bedroom with a sandwich for him.

"Thanks, Mom." Tom took the plate. "Thank you for standing up for me. It's all I've ever wanted to do, attempt the Puzzle Train."

"Me too!" she smiled at him.

"What?" Tom looked up from his food.

"I've been applying for the adult version for years. I'd love to go on there! There's no way I was going to let Phil stop you."

"Thanks."

"You'd better not get into any more trouble at school though!"

"I promise, Mom!"

"You'd better get an early night so you are fresh and ready to go tomorrow morning. Oh, Tom, it's so exciting! I can't wait to see you on the train!"

He cleaned his teeth and was just about to get into bed when Phil entered his room. Tom's heart sank, what could he want now?

"I've been on a chat room. There's good money to be made if we sell your winning spot to someone else. People are bidding hundreds of thousands for a place on the train."

Tom looked at him in shock. How dare he try and sell his space on the train.

"The spot is transferable, I've checked the paperwork," Phil half grinned, half snarled. "Just think how that money could help your mom. A new kitchen, a holiday, a new car. You know her car has been giving her trouble. All you need to do is sign here." Phil held out a piece of paper and a pen. "You could actually do some good for a change."

The Puzzle Train was Tom's dream for as long as he could remember, but it would be amazing to help his mom out.

"She has been stressed," Tom muttered.

"Good lad, sign here." Phil pushed the paper towards Tom.

"Phil, I told you no," Trudi stood in the doorway to Tom's bedroom. "Tom, don't sign that."

"But what about the money?" Tom looked past Phil at his mom.

"That's not for you to worry about. We'll be fine." She snatched the piece of paper from Phil and ripped it up.

"Sleep well, Tom. It's the train tomorrow." She kissed him on the forehead. "You," she ordered, pointing at Phil. "Downstairs!"

Tom got into bed. Tomorrow his dream would come true, tomorrow he and his best friend would be on the Puzzle Train.

Chapter 7 - Breakdown!

Saturday morning dawned bright and Tom was awake early. He had hardly been able to sleep he was so excited. He was lying in his bed impatiently waiting for time to pass. He had tossed and turned to try and get back to sleep but without success. He checked his phone, it was 6.07 a.m. Just under four hours until the car picked them up. He wasn't sleepy, his head was full of the Puzzle Train.

He went to his window, opened his curtains and looked up and down the street. The row of houses, street lights, cars and trees all looked the same as usual, but Tom felt very different. This was a special day. He yawned and ran his hand through his hair. Phil's up early, he thought as he saw his slight figure in the front garden.

The front garden was small and much of it was given over to parking the cars. Tom watched as Phil popped the bonnet open of his mom's car. He's always checking the oil, Tom thought and went back to bed.

He typed a message to Isabelle. He was sure she would be asleep and wasn't expecting a reply.

"Hey, Issy, not long now. Can't wait."

Tom was shocked when his phone buzzed almost straight away.

"I know. Can't sleep," came the reply.

"How long have you been awake?"

"Hour or so."

"Me too."

"Four hours to go. Am doing homework to pass the time."

She's always doing homework, Tom thought to himself. He knew Phil would say that was why her grades were so good and he would then ask him why he couldn't be more like her. Tom gave Phil a whiny old lady voice in his head which made him chuckle.

After a few more minutes, Tom gave up trying to sleep. He was just too excited. He got up, showered and dressed. He chose his best jeans and a smart shirt as he wanted to look his best for when he met Marvin. He had his breakfast and played his favorite video game in his bedroom for a while.

At 8.02 a.m. he heard the familiar rattle of golf clubs as Phil pulled them out of the cupboard under the stairs.

"Good luck, love," he heard his mom say.

"Have fun, Trudi," said Phil.

Tom watched Phil load the clubs into his car and drive down the road.

"Great. He didn't try to ruin my day. That was good," thought Tom.

He was about to check the Puzzle Train website one more time before he left the house, when his mom came into his room.

"Oh good, you're dressed. We need to go to the mall quickly. Phil's asked me to get some things for him. After last night's argument, I said I would."

Tom nodded and went back to his laptop.

"Get your shoes on, you're coming with me," she added.

"Aw, mom!" Tom turned to look at her. "Can't I just stay here on my own?"

"Not today. Phil was on the internet trying to sell your spot last night and made me realise just how much in demand it is. You're coming so I can keep an eye on you."

"But I'll be fine here. Besides, the car will be here at ten."

"You're coming with me. We'll be back in plenty of time for you to get the car. If you keep arguing then I'll be shopping when the car comes and they won't let you go on your own."

Tom sensed defeat and so followed Trudi downstairs, put his shoes on and got in the car. He checked his phone, it was 8:15. He calculated quickly in his head, it was about ten minutes to the mall, maybe fifteen minutes shopping. They would be back in plenty of time. Tom relaxed in the passenger seat.

His mom had owned the car as long as Tom could remember. The grey seats were stained and fraying at the edges, the CD player didn't work and it had its own collection of squeaks, creaks and groans.

Trudi locked the front door and opened the driver's side door with a creak. The car seemed to wobble as she climbed in and she put the key in and tried to start it.

"Always the third time!" She winked at Tom as the first two turns of the ignition failed to start the car. On the third, the engine spluttered into life and she pulled out onto the road.

"Told you." She tapped Tom on the arm.

Tom kept checking the time as they drove. The traffic was light and they reached the mall in nine minutes. They walked into the store and found what they were looking for, another seven minutes. His mom stopped to grab a cup of coffee, which took six minutes.

They walked across the mall car park and back to the car. Plenty of time left, Tom thought as he got back in.

Tom's mom tried to start the car. She turned the ignition once. The car didn't start. It didn't start the second time either.

"Always on the third," she told Tom. Only this time the car didn't start on the third turn. Or the fourth. By the ninth or tenth, Tom was having a sinking feeling in his stomach.

"What are we going to do?" He stared at his mom.

"There's no answer from Phil." She tapped on her phone. "We'll call the towing company. Relax, Tom. We'll get you home in time to go."

Tom got out of the car as his mom made the call. He looked around at all the people driving their perfectly working cars and clenched his fists. Why today, of all days? went through his head. If Phil hadn't wanted his mom to go to the mall, he would be at home waiting, instead of being stuck miles away with no way of getting hold of anyone from the show.

What would happen if they turned up at ten to collect him and he wasn't there? Would they look for him? Would they wait for him? Or would they just select a backup from the thousands of other children who weren't lucky enough to be selected? He paced around the car as the thoughts of his chance of being on the show began to fade.

He pulled the business card out of his pocket. On one side, it said 'Lester Vince – Puzzle Train researcher.' On the other was the access code. He logged onto the website on his phone and entered the code. The driver was scheduled to be right on time.

"Hurry up, mom," he called in through the driver's window.

His mom was on the phone talking and put a finger to her lips to tell Tom to shush.

Tom sighed and looked around the car park again. Families with happy looking children, couples, people on their own all walking around on a sunny Saturday morning about to do their shopping.

He looks familiar, thought Tom as he squinted at the slightly built man with dark hair by one of the mall entrances. The man was still, as if he was waiting for someone. Is that Phil? It can't be, he's at golf, but Tom walked towards the man to get a better view.

As he got closer he was more and more convinced it was Phil. The man looked directly at Tom, then from side to side. Tom's view was obscured by a delivery truck and when it had past, the man was gone. There was no way of knowing for sure whether it was Phil or not.

Tom cursed under his breath and walked back to his mom's car.

She wound the window down manually. "We're in luck. The tow truck company has a vehicle close by. They'll be here soon."

His mom got out of the car and took a sip of her coffee.

"They'll take us to the garage. We'll leave the car and take a taxi home."

"The usual garage?" Tom asked.

"Yes, the usual one," sighed his mom. She was used to her car breaking down.

Tom worked out the time. The garage was close by, there would still be enough time to get home, with about fifteen minutes to spare.

"I'll book a taxi so it can meet us at the garage." She reached through the open window and tried the ignition once more. The car did not start.

"Did you see that man," Tom pointed, "by the entrance to the mall? He looked just like Phil."

"That's not possible, he's playing golf. Why would he ask me to come to the mall if he could come here himself?"

Yes, why would he, thought Tom. Unless he was desperate to make sure Tom wasn't at home and missed his lift to the Puzzle Train. He had seen Phil early this morning looking at the car. Could he have done something to the engine?

Tom showed his mom where he had thought he saw Phil.

"There's no one there now though."

"Too many video games, Tom," his mom said. "They've made you paranoid. Oh look, here's a tow truck now."

She waved at the driver and guided him to the stranded car. The tow truck driver introduced himself as Clint from PM towing and set about hooking the car to the tow truck.

"You'll take it to Mick's garage, on the corner of Acacia Avenue and Sixth?"

"I know the one, ma'am," Clint assured her as he checked the car was secure.

"Call me Trudi." And she and Tom clambered up into the truck beside Clint. He fired the truck into life and headed for the car park exit.

"I haven't heard of PM towing," said Trudi.

"We're a new business. PM is the owner's initials, but I've never met him."

They drove through the town slowly even though there wasn't much traffic. Tom kept checking the time on his phone. They stopped at a red traffic light and Clint checked his phone, and then indicated left.

"Shouldn't we go straight?" said Trudi.

"Umm … there's roadworks on Second Street. We'll need to take a detour." Clint turned as the traffic lights turned green.

That's not good, thought Tom. We'll just get home for ten, when the lift arrives.

They continued driving through the town. "This isn't the way," Trudi said firmly. "You should have turned back there. Where are you going?"

Clint ignored her, trying to keep his eyes on the road.

"Where are we going?" Trudi asked more firmly. "I'm going to call someone unless you answer me."

"Just a little further," said Clint. "We … er … usually work with Auto Motors on the edge of town."

"That's too far!" Anger was rising in Trudi's voice now. "We won't make it home for ten. Turn around and take us home. Now!"

Clint ignored her for as long as he could. Tom stared at the young man with bad teeth, imploring him with his mind to take them home.

"I can't, I have to take you to Auto Motors. It's … umm … company policy."

"Nonsense. You take me home now or I'm going to phone the police." She pulled out her phone and started dialling.

"There's no signal." Clint turned and looked at her, eyes wide.

"Pull over now!" Tom's mom screamed at Clint and started pulling on his arm.

"We're here," Clint pulled over at an old brick building, slamming on the brakes. The windows of the building were boarded up and weeds grew through the floor. There was a faded sign that once read 'Auto Motors'. Many letters had fallen off, so now it read 'to M t'.

Trudi almost pushed Tom out of the tow truck and stormed out and tried her cell phone again. There was no signal so she went to Clint who was hastily unhooking her car from the tow truck.

"What have you done? Where are we? Take us back, immediately."

"I can't." Clint lowered the car off the tow hooks. "He'll sack me." Fear was etched all over his face. "Or worse."

"Clint, don't worry, the police will help you." Tom's mom tried to remain calm. "Just take us home."

Clint pushed a button on the side of the truck and the hook lowered the car's front wheels to the ground. He rushed back to the driver's door, got in, slammed the door shut and started the engine.

"You stop there," Trudi shouted out at him through the window. She tugged on the door handle, but Clint had already locked it.

"I'm sorry," Clint shouted back as he pushed hard on the accelerator. The back wheels span gravel over the car and Tom's mom had to jump to the side to avoid being run over. The truck rejoined the road with a loud growl from the engine and drove off into the distance.

Tom watched the truck disappear around a bend, his hopes of appearing on the Puzzle Train disappearing with it. "What are we going to do now, mom?"

Chapter 8 - Limousine

"There's no cell phone service," Tom's mom almost shouted out in despair. "How can you find place in this day and age with no reception?"

Tom looked at his own phone which not only had no reception, but it told him they had only fifty minutes to get back home. He restarted it, still there was no reception.

He looked around the desolate area they were in. Close to the edge of town, a few run-down industrial buildings lined the road on one side, and on the other, a field. The road was single carriageway and judging by the pot holes, it was not well used.

"We're going to be here forever," Tom complained.

"Whining about it isn't going to help," his mom snapped at him. Tom turned his back on her, put his hands in his pockets and kicked at a stone.

"Sorry, Tom. That wasn't nice." His mom put a hand on his shoulder. "I guess I'm just as disappointed as you. I don't know what to do, we may have to walk."

"How long will it take us to get home?" Tom fought back a lump in his throat and wiped his eyes on his sleeve.

"We're on the wrong side of town." His mom looked down the road. "It must be at least two hours."

Tom's heart sank and a tear trickled down his face. He put his hands in his pockets and started walking. His mom joined him at his side as they walked down the road.

They walked in silence, deep in their own thoughts. Tom looked at feet, his shoulders slumped. His mom restarted her phone and held it aloft to try and get a signal.

"It's not fair!" Tom slapped his thigh. "All I ever wanted to do was go on the Puzzle Train."

"I'm sorry, Tom," his mom sniffed and wouldn't look at him.

This is Phil's fault, anger grew in Tom as he thought. If he hadn't insisted we go to the mall, we would be at home now waiting for the driver. He didn't want me to come. He did whatever he could to try and stop me applying. Was Phil involved somehow?

"What's Phil's last name?"

"Mulberry," answered his mom. She looked at him, her eyes were red. "Why?"

"The truck had Phil's initials on it. 'PM'. Don't you think that's weird?"

"Millions of people have the initials PM. I'm sure it's just a coincidence."

Tom looked at her and raised an eyebrow.

"And I'm sure you didn't see Phil at the mall," she said as if reading Tom's mind.

"What about the letters on the building. You could tell it said 'Auto Motors' but the only letters left were 'to M t." Tom paused to let it sink in with his mom. It didn't so he elaborated. "Tom T. Tom Treadwell. My name."

"Oh Tom. Now I'm sure that is a coincidence." They continued walking in silence, Tom's legs were beginning to get sore, but at least they were coming into a busier part of town. None of the few cars they saw would stop for them though.

"I'm going to miss it." Tom swallowed hard at the lump which returned to his throat. "The biggest adventure ever and I'm going to miss it. It's ten now. The car will be waiting outside our house and we're miles from home. Lester said don't be late and we're going to be late."

"Maybe the car will have to come this way to get to the station," his mom suggested, smiling half-heartedly.

Tom's legs started hurting and he was convinced he could feel blisters on the soles of his feet. He wasn't used to walking so far. They reached a bus stop and Trudi agreed that they could sit for a while.

"We should have signal by now." Trudi held her phone up. "This is a residential area, plenty of houses. I don't understand it."

Tom restarted his phone again and slumped into the hard-plastic seat of the bus stop. They were now twenty minutes late. Was the car still waiting for them? Isabelle was probably already on her way. Would they film the episode with five? Or was there a backup puzzleteer ready to take his place?

"At least it's not raining." His mom looked up to the sky where patches of blue poked between the clouds.

A few cars drove past, but no buses. Trudi started looking at the timetable which was attached to the side of the bus stop.

"We could wait here. There's a bus that will take us to the church on Green Street. It's only ten minutes from there to home."

Tom shrugged and mumbled in agreement. It didn't matter to him whether they spent all day out now.

The minutes dragged as they waited for the bus in silence. Tom was on his phone and didn't notice the limousine coming up the street until it had stopped beside the bus stop. The driver got out and walked around the car.

"Ms Treadwell?" he asked and touched his peaked cap. "And you must be Master Treadwell.," He held out a hand covered in a leather glove for Tom to shake.

"Tom," nodded Tom and he shook the driver's hand.

"Lovely to meet you. Always happy to meet a fan of the show." The driver smiled at Tom, his small dark eyes seemed to sparkle as he did.

"Who are you?" Tom's mom frowned at the driver. "How do you know us?"

"I'm Jenkins your driver." He bowed towards Tom's mom and walked towards her, hand outstretched in greeting.

Tom thought he would be able see his reflection in the driver's shoes, they were polished so brightly. His black suit was immaculate and his bright white shirt matched the white hair poking from the bottom of his cap. It was so neat, it seemed there wasn't a single strand out of place.

"The Conductor sent me. I'm here to take you to the Puzzle Train."

Tom's heart leapt. He was going to be able to take part.

"We've had a very weird morning," Trudi told him as she shook his hand quickly and then folded her arms. "How can we trust you? And how did you know we were here?"

Jenkins smiled and reached into his inside jacket pocket. "Here you are, Tom, the Conductor asked me to give you this, just in case." He handed Tom a folded piece of paper.

"It's my application!" Tom read the print quickly. He went red when he read what he had written about the Conductor being an alien.

"There's no way he could have got this without being connected to the show." Tom showed his mom.

"But how did you know we would be here?" Trudi persisted.

"I had explicit instructions from the Conductor," explained Jenkins as he pulled a cell phone from his other jacket pocket. "Here's your address." He had a map app open. He swiped to a note. 'If they're not home, head to the west end of town. They may be walking.'

"The Conductor had a feeling you'd have some bad luck this morning."

"You've got reception on your phone. We've had none all morning." Tom held up his phone to show Jenkins.

"I think you may have a bug. The limo has Wi-Fi and an anti-virus. You don't have to even get in, just stand next to it."

Tom went and stood next to it. It was at least twice the length of most other cars, black and as shiny as the driver's shoes.

Trudi looked at the driver. "I just don't understand how you knew where to find us."

"The Conductor is a very clever man. Tom, is your phone working now?"

Tom nodded as several messages now came through on the screen.

"Log on to the Puzzle Train website and enter the code that Lester gave you last night."

Tom did as he was told. The website gave him details about Jenkins, and a picture. As well as the registration number and details about the car, including its current location. Trudi checked them thoroughly before folding her arms once more.

"No. I still don't get it. We're taken by a false tow truck to the wrong end of town and then you show up like you expected us to be here. There's something weird going on."

"But, mom. This guy is going to take us to the Puzzle Train."

"But nothing. I don't like this. Come on, Tom. Let's keep walking."

Tom looked at the driver and the limo with wide eyes, but wouldn't walk away.

"Wait!" Jenkins called after Tom's mom. "I think you may be able to talk to someone who might convince you this is real."

Jenkins pulled his phone from his pocket and pushed the screen.

There was a dialling tone, followed by a "Hello" from a familiar voice.

"Hello, sir," Jenkins spoke into his phone. "Sorry to trouble you, but would you mind talking to Ms Treadwell?"

"Of course, no problem," came the reply.

Jenkins handed the phone to Trudi, Tom leaned over to look at the screen as well. There was a familiar wide grin and blonde curly hair.

"Marvin!" cried Tom, unable to hide his delight.

"Good morning. Is everything alright?" asked Marvin.

"Umm ... good morning ... Marvin. Umm Mr. Station Master." Tom's mom looked at the screen and ran her hand through her hair. "We're having a very strange morning."

"Well it's about to get awesome. Soon you'll be here with me attempting the Puzzle Train." Marvin moved his phone to show Tom and his mom the scene at the station.

"Look, here's the train. People are busy setting up." On screen was a man carrying a reel of cable. "Here's the waiting room, just waiting for you." Marvin chuckled at his own joke.

Tom's heart skipped a beat, a weight was lifted from him.

"That's great, but what time is it?" asked Trudi.

"What?" Tom looked at her in disbelief.

"I have to check it's not pre-recorded," she replied out the side of her mouth.

"It's about ten twenty-five." Marvin was looking at his watch, which he then showed to the screen.

"I'm happy," said Trudi. Tom heaved a sigh of relief.

"See you soon," Marvin beamed. "TTFN."

"Great." Jenkins took the phone, placed it back in his pocket and opened the door for her. "Let's get going. The Conductor hates to be kept waiting."

Tom and his mom climbed into the back of the limo, Jenkins closed the door and got into the driver's seat.

"My messages have just come through as well," Trudi showed Tom. The leather seats inside the limo formed an L shape along the back of the car and on one side. On the other side there was a TV and a fridge. Tom first sat and then lay down on the comfortable seat. His mom sat on the back seat.

There was a screen blocking their view of the driver but his voice came through a speaker.

"We'll arrive in approximately thirty minutes. Help yourself to drinks from the fridge and feel free to use the on-board information system."

The limo drove back through the town and Tom looked out of the tinted window as the familiar shops, buildings and then his school went past. Eventually they stopped at a traffic light just before the motorway.

"Ha, look," said Trudi holding out her phone so Tom could see a picture of a golf course. "Phil just sent this to me. You see, he is playing golf."

Tom wasn't going to argue. He was on his way to the Puzzle Train. He messaged Isabelle and told her about his morning.

"Are you excited about your day?" Jenkin's voice came through the speaker.

"Oh, yes, I can't stop talking about it with my best friend. Sometimes she says I talk too much about it and should try finding other things to talk about. Have you met the Conductor? What's he like?"

"Everyone says how mean and secretive he is. I've never met him. He has his own driver."

"He seems mean on the show, but I don't think he is. Well, not in real life. It does make the show better. Marvin is great and funny, but the Conductor is the genius. He devises the best puzzles!"

They chatted for a while and Tom told the driver how he had worried his answer to the tie break question wasn't good enough. He then told the driver all about Isabelle's answer and how he had wondered for a while whether the Conductor didn't exist, and how he had felt down about that.

"I phoned Gran, I was so worried about the answer I had put."

Tom's mom looked at him in surprise. "Did you? You never told me!"

"And what did your gran say?" asked the driver.

"She told me it is what it is. If I went with what I felt then at least I was true to myself. If I didn't get on the show, then it wasn't meant to be. Can we visit her over the summer? I miss her."

"We'll see," promised his mom, holding his hand.

Tom left it for a second, but then with an, "Ugh, Mom," he pulled his hand away.

Tom and the driver chatted for most of the journey. About Phil, their morning, Isabelle and his gran. The car pulled off the highway and onto a smaller road and eventually drove into another town.

"Is it far to go?" said Tom.

"Nearly there," the driver replied.

The car drove through the town for a while, and eventually turned right down a slope and into an underground car park. They stopped at a security gate, where the guard on duty waved them through.

After being in the sun, Tom's eyes took a few seconds to adjust to the relative darkness of the car park.

"Jenny's waiting for you. You're right on time." Jenkins brought the car to a halt next to a glass door. The light in the room behind the door was a lot brighter than the light in the car park and Tom could through to a woman staring at her watch.

Jenkins got out of the car and opened the door for Tom and his mom to get out.

"Thank you." Trudi studied Jenkins

"You're welcome," said Jenkins. "And good luck to you, young Tom." Tom shook his hand and thanked the driver but his attention was on finding Isabelle and telling her more about his strange morning.

Jenny pushed one of the glass doors open impatiently and waved Tom and his mom to come through. She had brown hair tied back in a ponytail and was carrying a clipboard. On her head she wore large headphones which joined up to a microphone, through which she was talking to someone. She was wearing a blue hoodie with the Puzzle Train logo and blue jeans. Tom saw the logo and excitement flooded through him.

"Yes, Larry, they're here … yes, the last ones … little boy. Must be …" she looked at her clipboard, "…Tom and Trudi Treadwell. Hi, are you Tom?"

Tom nodded.

"Awesome. And you must be Trudi. Welcome to the Puzzle Train." Jenny shook their hands and then led them down a corridor.

"OK, let's go. Follow me … Yes, Larry… bringing them up now."

"The Conductor runs a very tight ship and we don't like to upset him by being late. I'm taking you to the other puzzleteers now. 11.30 a.m. 'Meet and Greet'," She held up her clipboard and tapped it. "11.45 a.m. Orientation."

Tom looked at his phone. 11.28 a.m.

They took an elevator, to the next floor. The doors opened with a 'bing' and they followed Jenny down a corridor past closed doors on both sides.

At the end of the corridor, they turned left. Tom's eyes widened to the size of saucers and the hairs on his arms stood up.

There in front of him was a scene he had seen thousands of times. The Puzzle Train. The engine off to his left and then each of the six beige carriages. The carriage next to the engine had a purple 6 on it. The final carriage to Tom's right had a purple 1 on it. Directly in front of him was carriage 2.

Tom stared at it and felt small. The train seemed much bigger in real life than it looked on TV. The puzzles are in there, he thought to himself. Our puzzles. The Conductor has designed puzzles for us and they are in those carriages now waiting for us! He grinned from ear to ear.

Then Tom looked around at the rest of the station. There were things he had never noticed on TV. The platform was lined with all sorts of TV production equipment, including two massive cameras against the wall on each side of the corridor Tom had just walked through. The station roof was far above him, much higher than he had expected. To the left, past the engine, he could see the train tracks stretching away, lined on both sides by buildings.

People were bustling around on the platform. They all wore similar hoodies to Jenny's with the Puzzle Train logo on. They seemed to be doing their last-minute checks before the show started, checking the train, and the sound equipment. One man was tapping away on a laptop and one was looking at a screen checking the lighting. All of them ignored Tom except for a man with scruffy brown hair who smiled quickly and then looked back down at his clipboard as he walked off.

"Come on, Tom!" called Jenny over her shoulder. "In here, we're two minutes behind schedule."

Jenny opened a door on the platform opposite carriage one that led to a corridor with three doors. "Trudi, please wait here on the platform and I'll join you again soon. Tom, come with me through this door to meet the other puzzleteers."

Chapter 9 – The Station

"Hi, everyone. This is Tom. Tom Treadwell. Say 'hi' to your fellow puzzleteers, Tom." Jenny led Tom into a small, brightly-lit room

"Hi," said Tom and waved his hand nervously.

Jenny introduced the others to him. Isabelle was talking to Holly Grayson, who seemed very relaxed. Harvey Roberts and George Irveine were having an animated discussion about the Puzzle Train, but stopped to greet Tom. Harvey was at least head and shoulders taller than Tom and skinny with long brown hair that he kept brushing out of his eyes.

George's voice was shaking with nerves as he greeted Tom and crossed the room to shake his hand, but he tripped over a plastic orange chair and fell to his knees.

Harvey burst out laughing. Shaun, the final boy, ignored him, his sullen expression unchanged as he stared at his feet. Both the girls were shocked and asked if he was all right. Tom was taken aback but didn't quite know what to do.

Jenny covered her face with her clipboard. "Please tell me he's all right," her voice muffled and slightly stressed.

"I'm fine," said George in a rather small voice.

"Up you get, mate." Harvey was still chuckling and held out his hand to help George up. "You'll be all right." George went pink in the cheeks and dusted himself down.

"Thanks," said George. "Dad's always saying I must be the clumsiest boy in the world."

When Jenny introduced Shaun Hegerty to Tom, the boy looked up briefly, frowned, and then looked back down at his feet. He had narrow eyes with black lines underneath them, and a thin pale face topped with jet black hair.

"Er," said Jenny, taken aback by Shaun's rude response.

"Right, I will leave you to get to know each other and then I will come and fetch you at eleven forty-five for orientation. Help yourselves to cookies and drinks." She gestured to a table against the wall and left the room.

"Aren't you excited to be here? I was so thrilled when Marvin read my name out," Holly asked Shaun as she turned to him.

Tom admired the way Holly spoke to Shaun. He didn't often know what to say when people were in a bad mood. Usually that was Phil and the best thing to do was leave the room.

"No, I'm missing football training to be on this show!" Shaun replied still looking down at his feet.

"But you can do football training any time." Tom offered encouragement. "There's only one chance to be on the Puzzle Train."

"I don't even watch it. I don't know what it's about!" Shaun got up to go to the table and grabbed a biscuit.

"But if you don't watch then why did you apply?" asked Isabelle.

"I didn't. It was my stupid little brother who applied. But he was too young to be on the show, so when he won he was so upset he wasn't allowed to take part. My mom made me come instead!"

He put on a fake whiny voice.

"Shaun's too young so you'll have to go instead, Darren, otherwise your little brother will be s-o-o-o-o disappointed!"

It was obvious to Tom, now Shaun was standing, that the other boy played a lot of football. He looked sporty and athletic, and was dressed in shorts and a replica football top. Tom thought Phil would just love a stepson like that.

"So now you have to pretend to be Shaun?" said Harvey, smiling.

Shaun half nodded and ate his biscuit.

In the minutes that followed, the children chatted, finding out how long they had been fans of the show and where they came from. Only Shaun was silent.

The door opened and Jenny walked back in, clipboard in hand. She seemed breathless as if she had been running.

"Attention please, everyone, it's eleven forty-five and time for orientation," she panted.

"What's orientation?" Harvey asked, with a mouthful of biscuits.

"Well, what we do is show you around the set, so you can see everything. You'll also meet Marvin so you can chat to him before we start filming. But first you need to change into your jumpsuits."

Behind Jenny was a man carrying six green jumpsuits. They were all the same, except each had a name embroidered on the front. Jenny took the suits and handed them out and directed the six children to their locker rooms.

Tom grabbed his jumpsuit and rubbed his fingers over the embroidered 'Tom'. He felt his heart skip a beat and he had to take a deep breath.

"Put your clothes, phones and anything else you might have with you in the lockers provided and you'll get them back at the end of the day. You can keep the jumpsuits as a memento. Quick as you can, please. The Conductor doesn't like to be kept waiting." She clapped her hands to hurry them along.

"Oh, and I do hope you are all wearing suitable shoes." With that she started looking at the six children's feet. "Mmm, yes, good, that's OK." She was muttering under her breath. "Good, all footwear is acceptable."

In the locker room, Tom was eager to get on with the experience and threw open his locker, kicked off his shoes and trousers and started to pull on his jumpsuit. He could see Harvey and George doing the same with massive grins on their faces. Shaun was getting changed with much less enthusiasm, muttering under his breath about it being stupid or how he was missing football training.

"Don't mind Mr. Grumpy," said Harvey. "How amazing is this place?"

"It's awesome," agreed George.

Shaun looked up at him with a scowl on his face.

"It's even better than I could have hoped," Tom said.

"I can't wait to meet Marvin."

"Nor can I."

The girls also changed quickly and rushed outside. "Great, you're all ready," said Jenny. "You can give the locker keys to your parents in a minute… Hang on, wait, where's…" she looked at her clipboard. "Where's Shaun?"

She rapped on the locker room door. Shaun opened it, strolled out and thrust his hands in his pockets. Tom thought he wasn't going to do many puzzles with his hands in his pockets.

"Great, all here, follow me," Jenny turned around and walked back down the corridor towards the platform. She checked her clipboard and then her watch and muttered under her breath, "Still two minutes behind," and shook her head. "Come along, quickly now."

They hurried onto the station platform, turned left and walked towards the engine, pointing out towards outside and the destination station ninety minutes down the tracks. Tom couldn't help but gaze at the dark blue engine. It was far bigger than he had imagined.

"Up here," Jenny called as she climbed a metal staircase. She waited at the top, on a balcony overlooking the station outside a closed door.

"This is the master control room," she announced proudly when all the children had made it to the top of the stairs. She opened the door.

It was the most amazing room Tom had ever seen and they all stared round them in disbelief. Even Shaun stopped looking grumpy.

A massive screen ran the whole length of one wall. It was divided into small screens showing highlights from previous weeks, shots of the waiting room, the car park, the platform and the technical teams making last minute adjustments.

In front of the screens was a huge desk full of buttons and switches, keyboards, dials, computer screens, knobs, joysticks and other controls. There was a row of four leather chairs along the desk. Behind these was another row of chairs where the children's parents were sitting, chatting and drinking coffee.

"The producers will be watching you on these screens as you progress through the train. From there they will decide which camera angles and shots will be used on TV. They can change any camera angle from here, and zoom in and out," Jenny explained.

"There're no pictures of the inside of the train," George observed.

"We can't give the puzzles away, can we?" Jenny huffed. "Your parents will also be watching you in the train from here. Give them your locker keys and say goodbye for now as you won't be seeing them again until after the show."

Tom gave his mom his key. She grabbed him and hugged him.

"Good luck, I'm so proud of you!" She kissed him on the cheek.

"M-o-o-o-m, not in front of the TV lady," said Tom, although as he looked round he could see the other parents doing the same, so he didn't feel so bad.

Suddenly the screen changed. It was no longer thirty individual screens but one massive one, showing just one picture of an extremely large face. Marvin! His grin was wide and his eyes were sparkling.

"Now, Jenny," Marvin's voice came through a speaker system that Tom couldn't see. "What are you doing with my youngest ever puzzleteers?"

"I'm just showing them around." Jenny tapped her clipboard. "Orientation."

"Well, hurry up and bring them, I can't wait to meet them."

"Yes, Marvin, we were just about to leave."

"Great, TTFN!" Marvin waved, and the giant screen once more turned back into thirty smaller screens.

The children followed Jenny out of the room and down the stairs, followed by a chorus of 'goodbye' and 'good luck' from their parents.

"Waiting room now," Jenny called over her shoulder as they walked back down the length of the platform. "Let's go and meet Marvin."

Five of the six children were extremely excited, having seen the waiting room week after week as Marvin interviewed each team of puzzleteers before they embarked on their journey.

Tom stared at the carriages as they walked past them, wondering what kind of puzzles were waiting for them. At the end of the train, they turned left and saw the waiting room in real life for the first time.

The building was made of pale beige bricks topped with a red tile roof which extended beyond the walls and was supported by ornate wrought iron supports. There was a green door and a large window on its right with a bench underneath it. Either side of the door was a hanging basket overflowing with flowers and ivy trailing down towards the grey concrete floor.

As they approached, the door was flung open and Marvin stepped through. He stood in the doorway, hands outstretched, feet apart and that all too familiar grin on his face. He was dressed in a bright yellow shirt with a white collar and pink trousers.

"Well, hello, my young puzzleteers. And what an excited looking bunch you are!"

Isabelle and Holly started giggling with excitement. Tom, George and Harvey were slapping each other on the back.

"Who's this guy?" said Shaun.

"This is Station Master Marvin! He's the host! The presenter! He's awesome. Haven't you ever watched the show? I mean not even to see what would happen? Weren't you even curious?" Harvey almost yelled with frustration.

"Don't worry, Harvey. He'll soon pick up on everything. Nothing is going to stop me having the best time ever!" said Tom.

"I said hello, young puzzleteers," Marvin called out more loudly and with even more enthusiasm.

"Hello, Marvin," called all the children except Shaun.

"That's much better. Now come on into the waiting room."

The six of them followed Marvin inside. Jenny entered last. Tom and the other puzzleteers looked round in wonder and excitement. Tom noticed many things he had not seen from watching TV. The pattern on the brickwork, the timetables on the counter, the old-fashioned tills in the ticket office and even the pot plant in the corner of the room.

"Gather round, gather round," Marvin waved his arms around in a circle so hard he almost could have taken off. "That's it, form a semi-circle. Great."

Marvin looked at the happy expectant faces in front of him. He stopped when he got to Shaun.

"Oh dear, you look a grumpy Gus. What's wrong?"

"I had football training this morning."

"Football training! Oh dear. Well, yes, I can understand that must be important, but how often is it you get to be on TV in front of millions of people?" He grinned at Shaun.

"Well, I s'pose," said Shaun

"That's a good lad," said Marvin. "I get to be on the TV in front of millions of people every week and trust me it's the best thing EVER!"

Behind the puzzleteers, Jenny coughed and looked at her wrist as a signal to Marvin that he needed to hurry up.

"Right!" Marvin said, a little more serious now. "We can't keep the Conductor waiting so let's move it along. This is your orienteering time. What that means is that you have the chance to find your feet around the station and with each other. When we start filming, I will come in here and have a quick chat with you all so we can introduce you to the folks at home. So, you have a little time to think about what you can tell me. Keep it simple like, my name is… I'm from so and so town and I enjoy doing such and such when I'm not at school. Everyone got that?"

Everyone nodded, even Shaun.

"That's great. Then after we've had a nice little chat, there will be a few minutes while the technical team finishes things off and then we will pack you off to the train to start your adventure. Now, are there any questions?"

Tom put his hand up nervously.

"Yes, young man," said Marvin.

"Where's the camera in here?" Tom asked shyly.

"Ah, yes. There will be a cameraman waiting with you here when I join you after we record the introduction to the show. When you get in the train, all the cameras are remotely operated. You'll probably hardly even notice them."

"Oh, and you will be able to watch us filming the introduction to the show as there will be a monitor in here," Jenny added.

"Now, are there any more questions?" asked Marvin.

"When do we meet the Conductor?" blurted out Harvey excitedly. "I really want to see him."

"Ah, yes, well of course, the Conductor is in his office at the destination station, which is at a secret location. If you get through all our puzzles today you will meet him. I'm sure he will appear and make a comment or two when we are chatting in here later. He usually does." Marvin grinned and winked at Harvey.

Marvin went to each of the children and shook their hands. "Best of luck. I'll see you next when we're recording our interviews for the show. Just relax and enjoy it. Nothing to worry about. Just pretend we're having a little chat in your living room. We have spare time built in just in case we need to record anything again."

"Phew," said Isabelle. Tom thought the same.

"See you all soon. TTFN!" Marvin said happily as he left the waiting room waving. He walked past the train and out of sight.

"All right, everyone, how are you all feeling? OK?" Jenny was looking at her clipboard and didn't wait for a reply "We're just about running on time. Let's complete your orientation."

Jenny showed them around the rest of the studio. There were a few offices, a make-up room, technical department, the costume department, a store room, the toilets and the canteen where the tour ended.

Jenny looked at her watch and then down at her clipboard.

"You've got fifteen minutes and then I'll come back and get you ready to start filming. So now is the time to go to the toilet and get something to eat and drink if you want to."

"Is it free?" said Harvey, licking his lips.

"Yes, help yourselves, but I wouldn't have too much if I were you. You just never know what the Conductor has in store for you." She scuttled from the canteen looking at her clipboard once again.

"What's on that clipboard that's so interesting?" said Isabelle.

The canteen was a large room, lit with fluorescent tubes and set back from the platform. There was a selection of snacks spread out behind a glass-fronted counter and some jugs of juice. Tom was drawn to the snacks. In all the excitement of the day, he realised he hadn't eaten since his early breakfast. There were sandwiches, filled rolls, muffins and doughnuts.

"Hello, dear."

The voice came from a kindly grey-haired woman behind the counter wearing an apron, a hair net and a kindly smile. "You look hungry." Her name badge read 'Maude'.

The children each took some food and drink and sat at a table together. They were quiet and Tom took the time to look at them all. My fellow puzzleteers, he thought. Isabelle was looking nervous, nibbling on a sausage roll. Harvey was eating as if he hadn't eaten all day, his plate piled high with sandwiches and doughnuts. He kept brushing his hair out of his face. George was way too nervous to eat. His eyes seemed the size of saucers as they darted around every inch of the canteen. Holly was looking by far the calmest of them all, humming gently and looking around the canteen taking everything in. Shaun was just looking grumpy and bored. He pushed the food around on his plate and then got up to go to the rest room.

"Holly, what will you ask for if we win?" Isabelle broke the silence.

"I'd love to take my whole family on holiday. I'd book a theme park for the day just for us so they'd be no queues."

"Nice," Isabelle nodded. "I'd love a pony, and gymnastics equipment and a room to put it all in."

"I'm going to ask for all the latest games consoles and all the games to go with them and a massive TV and sound system," said Harvey.

"I really want a speedboat," said George. "No, wait, a jet ski. No, wait, I'll have both."

"What about you, Tom?" asked Harvey.

Before Tom could answer, Jenny and her clipboard came into the canteen and interrupted. "OK, guys. It's nearly time to start the show. But first we have to take you to make-up!"

Shaun arrived back in the canteen.

"You've got to be kidding. Make-up?" Shaun glared at Jenny.

Isabelle and Holly looked thrilled. The other three boys looked at each other with horrified expressions.

Jenny laughed. "Just a little to stop the lights glaring off your faces."

She waited with them in the make-up room, where the two girls chatted excitedly and the four boys screwed up their faces.

"That's better. Don't you look pretty?" Jenny smiled at the children.

Shaun snorted and muttered under his breath.

Jenny checked the time. "All ready to go'"

Tom's heart leapt.

"Follow me. It's time to start filming!"

Chapter 10 – Accident!

They followed Jenny back to the waiting room, where they found a cameraman waiting for them and in the corner, as Jenny had said, there was a monitor.

"Hi there," the cameraman said cheerily.

"This is Steve. The best thing to do is try and pretend he isn't there. You'll soon get used to him," said Jenny.

"Hi Steve," the children chorused.

"I hope you've thought about what you are going to say to Marvin when he comes and talks to you," said Jenny.

"Oh yes, definitely," said Isabelle.

"Great. And what about you, Shaun?" Jenny frowned at him as he thrust his hands in his pockets.

"I suppose so," muttered Shaun.

"This is your chance to be on prime-time TV. Best you make the most of it," said Jenny. "We had thousands of entries and you six were chosen for a reason."

She crouched down and turned the screen on. There was a picture of one of the carriages.

"This is a live feed from the main camera out on the platform." She looked at her watch. "OK, guys, this is where I leave you for a little bit. You'll be able to watch Marvin record his introduction."

A man came into the picture. He was wearing headphones and had a clipboard. He completed some checks, put his thumbs up and walked away.

Shaun was looking around the waiting room impatiently. He tried to put his head through one of the ticket windows but it was too small.

"So much waiting around. I'm bored." He scouted around the waiting room for something to play football with, but there was nothing.

"Shhh, here comes Marvin," said Holly.

Even Shaun turned to look at the screen as Marvin and his huge grin came into the picture. He was wearing the same yellow shirt and pink trousers he had on earlier, but had now added a bright red bow tie. The camera panned out and they could see that Marvin was at the far end of the station by the gleaming blue engine of the train.

"Good evening and welcome, puzzle fans. We have a first for you on this very special show. Six lucky children will attempt the Puzzle Train for the first time. They won their places by completing puzzles online and going through a rigorous selection process. Our very own Conductor reviewed their tiebreaker question to select the six he considered to be the most suitable puzzleteers."

Marvin started walking beside the train, past carriage six. He stopped at carriage five and turned quickly back to the camera.

"Now there's no change to the rules. Six carriages and an hour and a half to complete the puzzles. If they complete all six carriages in time, they then get a bonus ten minutes to take on the final station puzzle and, if they complete that, then the Conductor awaits them."

Marvin stopped and looked directly at the camera.

"How was that? Is everything fine? How's the sound?"

An unseen member of the production crew answered.

"All good, Marvin. Yes, we can move on."

"Thanks, Ant," said Marvin. "Can you see my bow tie? Look closely. It has pictures of little trains all over it." Marvin grinned widely as the camera shot zoomed in on his bow tie. He moved his hair out the way so the camera could get a good look.

"Great! Let's continue. Are you ready? Cool." Marvin gave the camera the thumbs up, composed himself and started talking again.

"I have spoken to the Conductor and he tells me that these carriages…" Marvin stepped towards carriage number five and patted it with the palm of his hand, "These carriages contain puzzles every bit as difficult as the ones for the adults. I can't wait to see how our young puzzleteers get on. S-o-o-o let's go and meet them."

Marvin checked again that everything was fine with his sound and his bow tie, then walked along the side of the train towards the waiting room with a spring in his step.

He stopped at the door of the waiting room, turned to look at the camera and they recorded a second introduction.

Not long now, Tom thought. He was still feeling excited and nervous at the same time. He looked at the others and could see they were also nervous. Only Shaun looked disinterested.

Marvin turned around and opened the door. He double-checked with Ant that everything was in order, looked at his reflection in the window and gave his bow tie a little wiggle to make it straighter.

Tom and the rest of the children stared at the open door in anticipation, but were disappointed to see Jenny enter.

"Sorry, guys, just me." She looked along the line of disappointed faces. "Marvin is going to come in and chat to you in just a minute. Please can you all stand in a row over there by the ticket windows?"

"In a row?" Shaun interrupted with a scowl on his face. "That's just like school!"

"Yes, Mr. Smarty-Pants," Jenny sighed. She waved her clipboard around directing the children.

"Marvin will talk to you one by one, Steve will be in that corner and you standing in a row will give us the best shot."

They rushed across the waiting room, jostling and pushing for the best position, until eventually they stood in an untidy row. Harvey gave George one last push, just for good measure, and then Jenny surveyed the line-up, tapping her teeth with her pen, deep in thought. Tom was sure this was the longest she had ever spent not talking. It wasn't long before she broke her silence and started moving them around.

"Harvey, you're the tallest. You stand here. Tom, you come here to the end. Holly, you move here…" She looked at the row of children in their green jumpsuits. "Yes, that's it… perfect. OK, Marvin will come in now. Try and look relaxed. Thanks."

She walked back out through the door.

"Marvin, they're all yours," they heard her say as she left the waiting room.

"Thanks, Jen."

This time it was Marvin who walked in through the door. He brushed his long hair back in an exaggerated manner, looked at Steve, the cameraman, and said, "And here they are, our youngest ever puzzleteers." He flung out his arm in the direction of the children. Steve panned along the line, before pointing his camera back at Marvin.

"Don't they look marvellous?"

Marvin came first to Shaun, "Hello there, young man. Why don't you tell us about yourself?"

"Hi there, I'm Shaun and I would rather be playing football!" He sneered at the camera.

Marvin laughed. "You mean when you're not watching the Puzzle Train?"

"No, I would rather be playing football now!"

Marvin had presented the show since it started, eleven years ago. He had met thousands of puzzleteers from all sorts of backgrounds, but as far as he could but as far as he could remember everyone had wanted to take part. Ever the professional though he gave Shaun a hearty handshake and wished him good luck.

At the other end of the line Tom was watching and listening with disbelief. He was sure they would edit Shaun's comments out of the show.

"And who do we have next?" Marvin smiled broadly at Isabelle.

"Hi, my name is Isabelle and I love the Puzzle Train. When I'm not watching, I enjoy doing gymnastics and my maths homework."

"Ah, Isabelle, Isabelle, Isabelle, well a combination of gymnastics and maths could certainly come in handy in the Puzzle Train!" Marvin chuckled.

"Hi, I'm George, and I really want to meet the Conductor," blurted George before Marvin had a chance to speak to him.

"Well, you certainly are excited, George, and we're excited to have you here. We're all hoping you complete the puzzles and make it through to meet the Conductor."

Suddenly, there on the wall behind Marvin the unmistakeable silhouette of the Conductor appeared. Sitting at his desk and wearing his brimmed hat, the waiting room seemed to instantly become colder.

"Who's this guy?" said Shaun, turning to Isabelle.

Isabelle turned to him and said, "Shh, it's the Conductor."

"Yes, Shaun, do be quiet! We've had enough talk of football." The Conductor's booming voice filled the room. He was much louder than Tom had expected.

Shaun started to reply but the Conductor spoke over him.

"Enough!" He yelled.

"Now, now, Conductor, they're only children," said Marvin.

"Marvin, you can shh as well," boomed the Conductor, "George!"

"Y-yes, Conductor?" George stammered a little.

"Do you think you are good enough to make it through the train?"

"I … I th-think so." George seemed to shrink and stepped backwards slightly.

"You'd better do more than think, young George! Just because you're children doesn't mean that the puzzles are easier! Now, MARVIN!"

"Yes, Conductor?" Marvin said politely.

"Get on with it now, Marvin. I want to see which one of them gets caught in a cage first! I think it will be George!"

"Oh dear, poor George. Just like the adult version, there will be cages waiting for our children, where they can get five, ten or fifteen-minutes punishment. Now let's meet the final three puzzleteers."

The Conductor's silhouette remained on the wall.

"Hi, I'm Harvey and I love the Puzzle Train and playing video games."

"And sandwiches by the look of it," laughed Marvin as he wiped some mayonnaise off Harvey's chin.

"Hi, I'm Holly and I like horse riding, drawing and the Puzzle Train."

"Well, Holly, I don't think there will be any horses on the train unfortunately. And finally, who's this on the end?"

Tom gulped. His mouth was dry. He was so nervous.

"I'mTomandiamreallyexcitedtobehere," Tom blurted out.

"Now, Tom, you'll have to talk a bit slower than that." Marvin smiled at him to try and help him to ease his nerves.

Tom remembered that his gran had taught him if he was nervous he should take a deep breath to help him calm down. He took a deep breath.

"Sorry, Marvin. I'm Tom and when I'm not watching the Puzzle Train on TV, I watch it on YouTube or I check the website or I talk about it with my friends."

"Wow, you sound like our biggest fan! Been *training* hard, Tom!" Marvin laughed at his own joke. Tom smiled broadly even though he was sure Marvin had used that pun at least a thousand times. At the other end of the line, Shaun groaned.

"Bye for now, young puzzleteers. I'm sure we'll be speaking soon," the Conductor said menacingly as his image disappeared from the waiting room wall. Jenny came back in the room.

"Great, guys. Good take. Now we'll film you going to the train."

"Aw right! Let's go!" George jumped up like he had been stung and started running, pushing past Jenny.

"Wait for me!" Isabelle ran after him.

Tom, Harvey and Holly started running too. Shaun wandered out of the waiting room, his hands in his pockets. Steve rushed out as quickly as he could, camera over his shoulder, trying to film them, but they had already left him far behind. Harvey sprinted and closed the gap to George.

George had a healthy head start and won the race. He leapt onto the first step at the back of carriage one, but his foot slipped and jammed underneath the second step. Harvey couldn't stop and clattered into the back of him, pushing George's foot further underneath the second step and banging his head against the gate. Harvey bounced off George and fell on the platform, with an 'oof' as the wind was knocked out of him. Tom tripped over Harvey and landed in a heap. Isabelle and Holly managed to stop in time. By now Shaun was clutching his sides roaring with laughter.

George wrenched his foot free from between the two metal steps with an agonising scream. He hopped backwards, trying to keep his balance, but tripped over Tom, landing on his bum on the platform, clutching his ankle, wailing in pain.

"Oh no, George, are you all right?" Jenny ran up to George and leant over him. George rolled up the leg of his jumpsuit. His ankle was already swollen to double its usual size. Jenny spoke into her microphone.

"Get a medic here quickly!"

Within seconds George's dad had run down from the control room. Seconds later two medics arrived and inspected George's ankle.

George hid his face in his hands and howled in pain as the medic prodded gingerly at his ankle.

"We need an ambulance. We have to get him to hospital to get this x-rayed." The medic looked up from George's ankle to Jenny.

"Right away." Jenny pulled her phone out of her pocket and dialled.

The other children gathered around looking on anxiously as George sat on the ground, hunched up in pain.

"The ambulance will be here in five minutes. It'll come in through the car park. Can you carry him down there?" Jenny asked the medics.

"Yes, we can," one of them said and the two of them lifted George up very carefully.

"But I want to go on the train," George complained, wincing as the medics lifted him.

"We need to get you to hospital. We need to see if your ankle is broken," the female medic explained gently.

"Dad, I want to go on the train!" George started crying as the medics carried him towards the elevators down to the car park.

"We need to get your ankle looked at, sorry son." His dad followed behind, smoothing George's hair to try and calm him down.

The remaining five children looked sadly at each other. George's wails stayed with them after he had disappeared out of sight.

"Poor George," said Holly. "What do we do now?"

Jenny was talking on her headset again. "Yes… I know … What? … With the five? … OK."

"Attention, please, guys." She addressed the remaining five children. "The Conductor insists that everything runs to schedule. There's no time to get a replacement so he says he will run the Puzzle Train with just five of you."

"Awesome!" exclaimed Harvey.

Tom breathed a sigh of relief but then felt bad for George.

"All right, all right," said Jenny, through gritted teeth. "We need to film that again for the show. All of you back to the waiting room and this time WALK calmly to the back of the train. I don't want any more accidents. Steve, you stay in the building and film them from there. Yes, Linda," she called out to a young woman operating a large camera. "You take that camera there." Jenny gestured with her clipboard to a spot half way between the train and the station building.

"Just keep calm and try not to take any notice of the cameras."

This time they walked as instructed. Tom was aware this was probably the last time he would be on the station so he had a good look around. As he walked towards the train, he couldn't help but look at the camera. He waved at it, his grin was almost as wide as Marvin's. Isabelle saw him wave and laughed and blew the camera a kiss as she walked past. Harvey wasn't going to be left out and saluted the camera as he past. Holly grinned and waved as well. Shaun walked past with his hands in his pockets looking miserable as usual.

They reached the stairs and the gate. This time there were no accidents. Jenny shrugged her shoulders but decided that it was probably the best she could hope for.

With a quick look at her watch and her clipboard she announced to the children, "That was great, guys." And then she said the words Tom had been so desperate to hear.

"We're ready to go."

The metal gate was unlocked and the five children climbed up the stairs and onto the back of the train. In front of them was the door to the first carriage. The poem that would give them their clue was covered up, the clock was set at ninety minutes. The cage door closed behind them.

"What's this?" said Shaun.

"We are on the back of carriage one. We're not allowed into the first carriage until we start moving, but to keep us safe they put us in this cage thing on the back of the train." Isabelle rolled her eyes as she was explaining. Tom had seen a similar look from her many times when he asked her for help with his homework.

Jenny looked at her watch and breathed a sigh of relief. Despite everything they were bang on time.

"Never work with children or animals," she muttered under her breath. Then she called out, "The train will depart in ten, nine. Get ready because when it leaves the station the first clue will be revealed. Six, five, four."

She looked down the length of the train where the driver was looking back at her from the engine. She held up three fingers,

Then two,

Then one.

Then she gave the driver the thumbs up and the train slowly started to pull away.

Chapter 11 - Boxes

Tom felt the train start to move with a jerk that pushed him back on the metal bars. He was aware of everything. His senses were heightened. He could feel the movement of the train on the track, hear the rumble of the engine and feel the wind on his face. To his left he could see the station beginning to pass by, the cameras, the people and the stairs to the control room where his mom was watching. He saw the man with the untidy brown hair look up from his clipboard, smile and wave.

He could hear the gentle click clack of the carriage wheels as they started off along the rails. In front of him, on the door to carriage number one, was the all-important first clue, just seconds away from being revealed. To its right were the two digital clocks, one on top of the other. In green numbers, one showed a minute, their thinking time for the clue, one showed ninety minutes, the total time they had on the train. His gran had said to him that when he was doing what he loved he would notice everything. He hadn't been sure what she had meant before, but now he understood. Isabelle was standing next to him and he nudged her with his elbow.

"This is it, Issy!" he whispered to her. He thought briefly of George and felt sad for him. He had been so close to achieving his dream.

The back of the train cleared the platform and moved into the open. As it did, the sun shone briefly on the children before being obscured by a tall building. Both clocks started to count down and the poem was revealed.

> Carriage one and ready to go.
> It's time now, children, to begin the show.
> Lots to do, but where to start?
> Not a club, and not a heart.
> Pick carefully and pick right;
> Or a cage will be your plight.
>
> Time remaining 90:00.
> Thinking time remaining 01:00

"What does that mean?" Holly blurted out.

"Sounds stupid," muttered Shaun.

Harvey glared at him and groaned.

"As my gran used to say, you're here now so you may as well enjoy it!" Tom gave Shaun a friendly pat on the shoulder and Shaun managed a half smile back at him.

"So, what do you think of the poem?" asked Harvey.

The first two lines just seem to be an introduction, Tom thought. What if I'm wrong though? Clubs and hearts could mean a pack of cards, but I'm not sure.

"I don't think there's anything in the first two lines," said Holly.

Isabelle agreed with her.

"Yes. The next line seems to suggest that this will take a lot of time. Which is no surprise."

"Clubs and hearts are suits in a deck of cards," said Harvey. "That leaves spades and… umm."

Tom could have kicked himself for not speaking up. Diamonds, he thought.

"Diamonds," said Isabelle. "Tom, what do you think?"

"Umm." He was unsure of himself. He often felt like this. He knew the answer but didn't want to say anything for fear of getting it wrong.

" 'Where to start,' though. What does that mean? What do we have to pick?" Holly interrupted.

Before they knew it, the minute had ticked away and the door slid open. All Tom had managed to contribute to the discussion was 'umm'. Swallow the nerves, speak up, he told himself.

Harvey was stepping through the door even before it was halfway open. The rest of them followed eagerly, even Shaun. The door automatically slid shut behind them.

"What are these? Post boxes?" Holly looked at the left wall of the carriage which was filled from floor to ceiling and front to back with grey boxes, just big enough to fit a hand in.

Yes, Tom thought. But why are there pictures on some of them? They're the suits from playing cards.

"What are these pictures on them?" asked Harvey. "Why are most of them blank?"

"There's numbers across the top. One to a hundred and fifty," observed Holly.

Shaun was showing no interest in the boxes at all and was looking around with his hands in his pockets. A glint on the right wall of the carriage caught his eye.

"There's symbols down the left." Isabelle counted. "Twenty. That means …," she did some quick mental arithmetic…. "three thousand boxes in total. How do we know which one to open?"

"And how do we open the boxes?" said Holly.

"Well, here's the key!" called Shaun. "This is easy, now we just open the door." There was indeed a key hanging from a hook in the wall which Shaun grabbed.

He went to the door to the carriage. That won't work, thought Tom, that's for one of the boxes. The fear that he might be wrong and sound stupid stopped him from saying anything. The key, of course, did not fit in the door.

"No, wait. That key will open one of these boxes," said Holly.

Tom ground his teeth together. He knew that.

"Which one?" said Harvey. "Is there anything on the key?"

"Nah, its plain." Shaun showed him the key.

"Where was it?" said Tom, relieved to finally speak.

Shaun pointed. Tom investigated the area but it gave him no clues whatsoever. There was nothing at all on the right-hand side of the carriage other than the hook that the key had been hanging on.

The five children stood around in silence. That key opens a box with either a spade on or a diamond on, thought Tom.

Shaun was huffing, tapping his foot. Holly shushed him.

Seconds past before Isabelle broke the silence. "Some of these boxes have pictures on which are suits from a deck of cards. The clue said not clubs and not hearts. We need to look for a spade or a diamond."

The five of them scanned the three thousand boxes. There were twelve clubs and six hearts which they ignored. They found five boxes with spades and nine with diamonds.

Shaun was knocking on the nearest box with his knuckles.

"That's only fourteen boxes. Let's just try them one by one!" And without waiting for a reply, he went to the nearest to him which happened to be a spade.

"Wait!" said Tom. It felt good to find his voice. "Stop!" He knew what happened when puzzleteers became impatient.

"DON'T!" he called desperately, but it was too late.

Shaun ignored him and put the key in the hole and turned. Straight away the carriage lights went out, a red light started flashing in a corner of the carriage and a siren sounded. When the lights came back on, barely two seconds later, Shaun was in a cage, looking extremely annoyed.

On the right wall of the carriage a giant timer appeared, showing briefly the number five in bright red light. Then it began to count down the seconds. 4.59 … 4.58.

"What's that? Get me out of here! What's going on?" Shaun rattled at the bars, his cheeks reddening rapidly.

"You have five minutes in the cage," Holly told him.

Shaun muttered something unhappily from the cage and started kicking it, which didn't help.

The Conductor's silhouette appeared on the right wall, his deep menacing voice echoed through the carriage.

"Ha ha ha, too impatient, young Shaun. Now you can have a time out to think. Next time for you it will be ten minutes."

Tom realised that he knew that was going to happen. He puffed his chest out and seemed to grow an inch. This was his only shot at the Puzzle Train. He suddenly realised that a lifetime of study and watching the show was now going to pay off.

"Of course," said Tom, "the poem said to pick right, the clue is always in the poem. Shaun, give me the key."

Shaun poked the key between the bars of his cage. Tom took it and went to the box.

"This box is the farthest to the right with a spade on," he explained. "It's one of the Conductor's classic clues, a double meaning, not just the correct box, but also the one on the right."

Tom shook a little and the key jammed in the lock causing some doubt. Was he sure? Yes, he was. This felt right. He turned the key, took a deep breath, and turned. With a loud click, the box opened.

"Well done, Tom," said Isabelle.

Holly clapped happily, and Harvey slapped him on the back.

"Nice one."

Tom swelled with pride; the appreciation from his fellow puzzleteers was far more than he had ever received from Phil or Mr. Griffon.

The box was narrow, but Tom was able to reach in with his fingers and pulled out another key. This one had a key ring with a white plastic label attached. The label was rectangular, about the same size as Tom's hand and printed on both sides.

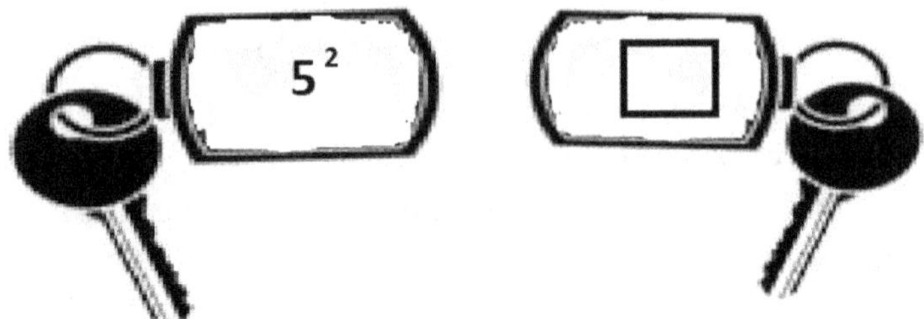

"That's five squared," pointed out Isabelle. "Twenty- five."

"Oh, look," said Harvey, "there's the square." He pointed to the symbol of a square to the left of the boxes, right at the top. Only he could reach up so high.

"Pass me the key," he said. He brushed his hair out of his eyes, went to column twenty-five and stretched up as far as he could, put the key into the lock and opened the box.

Inside was another key with another key ring. Harvey pulled the key out and showed the rest of the puzzleteers the plastic label.

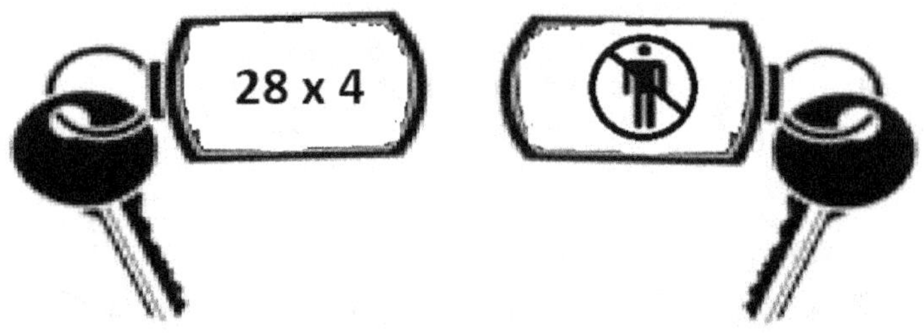

"Here's the symbol of a man." Harvey pointed.

"One hundred and twelve!" exclaimed Isabelle.

"Awesome, Issy! We just follow this across to a hundred and twelve," said Harvey and was about to put the key in the lock when Holly called, "Wait!

"It's a trick. The man has a line through him on the key ring but not on the symbols on the wall. I bet we need to use the picture of the woman instead."

"Are you sure?" said Harvey.

"Pretty sure… well, I think so," Holly said without any confidence.

"I agree with Holly. I'm sure that's why there's a line through the man," said Tom.

"You open the box on the woman row then," Harvey told Holly. "I'm not getting stuck in a cage if you are wrong!"

"Fine," said Holly and snatched the key from him. She entered the key in box and turned it quickly.

The box opened and Holly pulled out another key and key ring.

"Ha!" she said triumphantly to Harvey and stuck her tongue out at him.

"What's the clue, Holly?" said Tom.

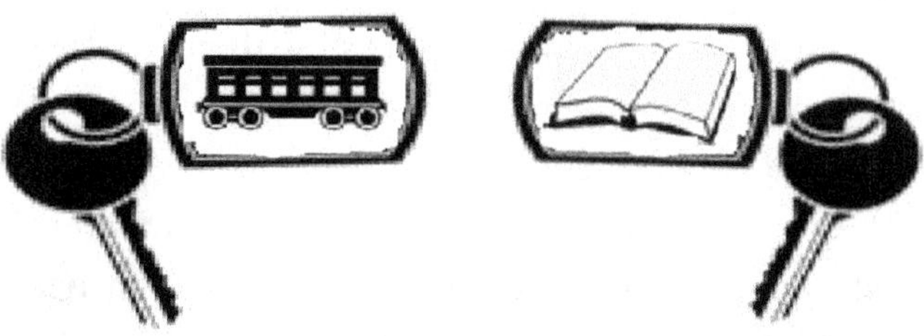

"There are no numbers on it. What do we do?" said Shaun from his cage.

"This is the Puzzle Train. It's not supposed to be easy," said Tom.

They looked down the symbols to see if there was a clue there.

"There's a book symbol and a train symbol." Holly pointed at the symbols as she spoke.

"But it's not a carriage," said Shaun from his cage.

"Well, a book could have any number of pages, any number of chapters," said Isabelle.

"What do we do?" said Harvey.

Tom took a deep breath and closed his eyes. What would he do if he was the Conductor?

The answer came to him, but before he could say anything Holly spoke.

"Six. We need book and six!"

"How do you know that?" Harvey said in disbelief.

"There are six carriages on the Puzzle Train," said Tom, "but I don't think that's right. I think it's one. There's only one carriage in the picture and we are in carriage one. I'm sure that's what the Conductor would be thinking when he made the puzzle."

On the opposite wall, the red counter ticked down to zero and Shaun's cage disappeared into the ceiling. Shaun stared at where the cage disappeared.

"Where the … did that go?" He stretched and then skipped around the carriage.

"Phew! I'd had enough of being in there."

"Do we go with one or six? I think they're both good answers but I'll go with Tom and say one. The amount of time Tom has spent watching Puzzle Train, I'm sure he's right," said Isabelle, "especially when he should have been doing his homework," she added with a smile. Tom smiled back at her.

"I'm with Holly. I think six," said Harvey.

"Shaun, what do you think? It's two against two," said Holly.

Shaun was still skipping around the carriage, enjoying his freedom. He stopped next to Holly.

"What do I think about what, Hols?"

"Hols?" Holly screwed up her face. "Is it one or is it six?"

"Umm, one I think. Yes, let's go with one." It was a total guess. "Definitely one!"

"He doesn't even know what we're talking about!" Harvey folded his arms.

"So that makes it three to two. Tom you can put the key in. I don't fancy getting stuck in a cage," said Isabelle.

"No problem, Issy. Pass me the key." Tom went to the far left of the boxes and put the key in the box where the book row and the first column met. The lock opened and Tom reached inside and pulled out the key and label.

Harvey and Holly both looked impressed and relieved that they didn't go with six as they would have been in a cage by now.

"A palm tree and what's that guy doing? Balancing a fish on his head?" said Harvey.

"That's a crown isn't it?" Shaun squinted at the picture.

"No, look. He's holding a rolling pin and a loaf of bread," said Tom. "He's a baker. A baker's dozen is thirteen."

Holly was looking down the symbols. "Elephant. A tree has a trunk and so does an elephant. A palm tree has a long trunk."

"There's no dog there is there?" asked Isabelle. "I was thinking of tree bark, giving us a dog."

Holly confirmed there was no dog. The key opened the box where thirteen and elephant met and another key with keyring was pulled out.

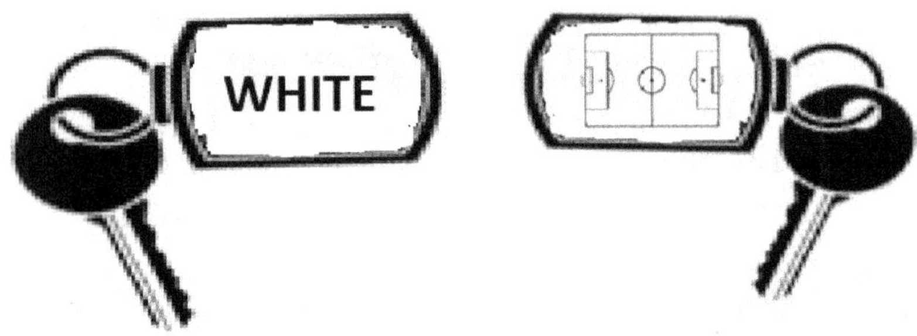

"That must be eleven, there're eleven players in a football team," said Shaun.

"But wait," said Isabelle. "You need twenty-two players for a game of football."

"Well done, Issy," Shaun gave her a friendly push on the arm. "It's a full pitch so I say we go with twenty-two."

"Yes, that makes sense," agreed Tom. "But what's white?"

"Umm, snow, a polar bear, bones?" said Holly.

"A football," said Shaun.

"Ice cream," smiled Isabelle.

"An elephant?" ventured Harvey.

"Are you sure?" said Shaun, his voice getting higher with disbelief. "White elephant? What does that even mean?"

"I'm sure I remember my gran saying something about a white elephant once," said Harvey.

"We've used the elephant and I don't see any of those others on this list," said Holly.

"The word 'white' is written in black. Do you think it's something black and white? Like a zebra or a penguin?" said Tom.

"I don't see any of those here either," said Harvey.

"Or a newspaper!" Shaun said jumping up with excitement.

"Nope, sorry, there's none of those here either." Holly shook her head.

"All right, then," said Isabelle getting frustrated, "what do we have on the symbols?"

They looked down the symbols, quiet, thinking, until suddenly Holly broke the silence.

"Oh, he's so clever," she said clapping. "That's a good one." She took the key from Tom and walked calmly over to the boxes and placed the key in the lock where a symbol of three stars and column twenty-two met. The box had a spade printed on it which Tom took as a good sign.

Holly turned the key and the box opened.

"But… what? How… huh. Hols, how did you know that?" Shaun finally completed his sentence.

"Yeah, come on, Hols, you're going to have to explain that," Harvey said with a hint of admiration.

"It's a play on words. I thought it might be a white knight, but I looked and there were no knight symbols. But the writing is in black and at *night* time it's black. Then I saw the stars which you can only see at night. I thought that has to be it!"

Shaun muttered something that sounded like "nuts" under his breath, but the other three collectively nodded and congratulated

Holly. She put her hand in the box. It was no surprise when she pulled out a key. But this time there was no keyring.

"Is that the door key?" said Isabelle.

They all rushed to the end of the carriage and Holly slipped the key in the door. It fitted and as they pulled on the handle, the door opened towards them.

There was another door behind it, plain white.

"I've seen this before," said Tom as a picture of a square emerged on the door. "What was the number for the square?"

Harvey ran back to the grid and looked at the opened box on the square symbol row. "Twenty-five," he called.

"Twenty-five," Tom repeated as clearly as he could. The square was replaced by a picture of a book. "The book?" he called to Harvey.

"One," Harvey shouted down the length of the carriage.

"One," Tom told the door. Next there was a spade from the playing cards.

"There isn't a spade row," Harvey called.

"The first box we opened had a spade on it." Holly's voice was several octaves higher than normal and she jumped up and down.

"Oh yes, here it is. One hundred and forty-four," Harvey shouted, then he added, "but there's a spade on the box in column twenty-two as well."

"Twenty-two or one hundred and forty-four?" asked Tom.

"One hundred and forty-four," said Holly. "I'm sure there would have been a picture of stars if the Conductor wanted number twenty-two."

"Yes," confirmed Tom. "I was thinking the same." He spoke to the door and this time Marvin's face appeared.

"You may proceed," said Marvin, with a smile. The door slid to the side, revealing the door to carriage two.

"Well done, guys, we made it through carriage one!" said Tom, thrilled.

Help Tom, Isabelle, Holly, Harvey and Shaun to identify which three lockers they need to open from the clues below:

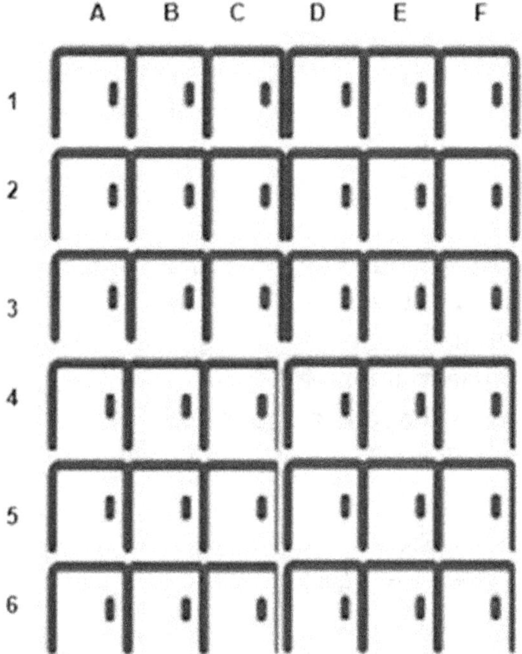

Who can get these clues faster?
The first is when something happens, but not after.
The second clue is where,
You change a view to cube from square.
The third clue is my suggestion.
What's the first part of Shakespeare's question?

Chapter 12 - Tiles

Welcome team to carriage two.
Six is the worth of the blue.
The blue is worth half a red.
Yellow on its own is four instead.
At least that's if the shape is a square,
If not, deduct one. Take care.

Time remaining 78:05.
Thinking time remaining 01:00

The minute clock started ticking down as soon as the poem was revealed. Twelve minutes taken in carriage one, Tom clenched his fists. Ninety minutes for six carriages gave them fifteen minutes per carriage. They were three minutes ahead of schedule.

"Hey, Issy, I think this could be a good one for you. It looks like there's some maths involved!" Tom nudged Isabelle with his elbow.

"Yes, but there's a lot to remember!" Isabelle bit her bottom lip.

"Why don't we each remember a line?" said Shaun.

"You seem happier now." Holly looked at Shaun and smiled.

"Tom was right. I'm here so I may as well try to enjoy it."

"Good to hear it," said Tom. "And that's a great idea."

"So blue is six, I'll take that one," said Harvey.

"Blue is worth half a red, so a red must be twelve. I'll take that," said Holly.

"Yellow is four. I'll have that one," said Shaun.

"And if it's not a square then deduct one. I'll remember that," Tom concluded as the minute ticked away and the door slid open. They all walked inside feeling confident they had a good plan.

They carriage was in darkness as they entered.

Shaun peered in through the door. "Where are the lights?"

"I've seen this sometimes, come in and the lights will come on." Tom waved for Shaun to come in. which he did.

The door slid shut behind Shaun and as Tom had predicted, the lights came on.

"Is it empty?" Holly said as they all looked around.

"What's on the floor? It feels like it's moving." Harvey bent down to investigate.

"Tiles." Isabelle held one up to inspect it. "The floor's covered in them."

"There must be thousands." Tom looked around the carriage in awe.

"This one has a green square on it." Isabelle showed it to Tom.

"Plastic and light." Tom took the tile and turned it over in his hands. "Like the tiles in my bathroom at home."

"The poem didn't mention green," Harvey added, looking over Tom's shoulder at the tile in his hand.

"There are other colors that weren't mentioned too." Holly called up from the floor. "Here's an orange star."

"The Conductor doesn't like to make things too easy," Tom muttered to Isabelle.

"What do we do, Tom? The poem didn't mention these extra colors." Isabelle's eyes were darting around the carriage. "What do we do?" she repeated.

Tom suddenly felt calm. All those years of watching the Puzzle Train were about to pay off. He put his hands on Isabelle's shoulders.

"Issy, calm down. The Conductor likes to play these tricks. I've seen loads of episodes where this sort of thing happens."

Isabelle took a deep breath and composed herself.

"We'll start with what we know. Work logically and see what happens,"

"See what happens?" Shaun interrupted. "What kind of plan is that?"

Isabelle ignored him and thanked Tom.

"It's the 'don't panic' plan." Holly held a tile in each hand. "And I like it." She beamed at Tom and then turned to Harvey. "What have you got there, Harvs?"

Harvey had totally missed the entire conversation. He was busy inspecting the left wall of the carriage.

"Look here," he said, pointing to a black panel with white symbols on it. "On the walls, there are puzzles – kind of like sums – look at the first one."

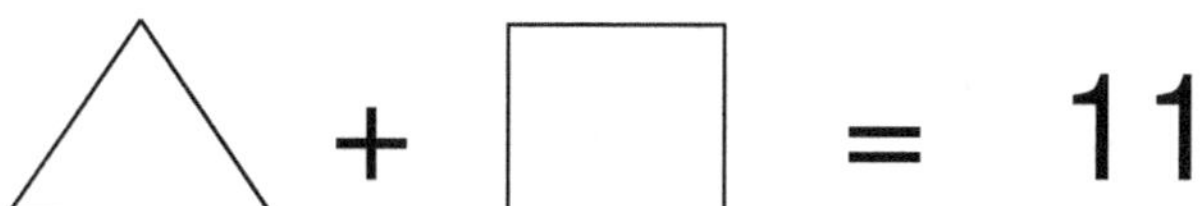

"This must be where we put the tiles." Harvey pointed to a bracket underneath the shapes.

"There's loads of sums." Isabelle turned around on the spot and counted. "Ten on each wall."

"This is going to take ages." Tom puffed out his cheeks. He was beginning to feel overwhelmed by the amount of work they had to do.

"Let's get going." Harvey tapped the triangle. "They won't solve themselves. We need eleven from a triangle and a square."

"It can't be red because they're worth twelve," said Holly.

"A blue square is six," said Harvey. "That leaves five. What's five?"

"Blue is six and any shape that isn't a square is one less, so we need a blue triangle. That's five," said Tom.

"Awesome. Let's find them then. A blue square and a blue triangle." Harvey was already scouring the floor around him for the right tiles.

"Blue square!" Holly held the tile aloft.

"Triangle here!" Shaun passed the tile to Harvey.

Harvey slotted the tiles into the correct brackets in the wall. They heard a 'ting' sound and the puzzle was bathed in a green light.

"What happened?" said Harvey.

"Green is good, I think. Green for go!" said Tom. "Let's go!"

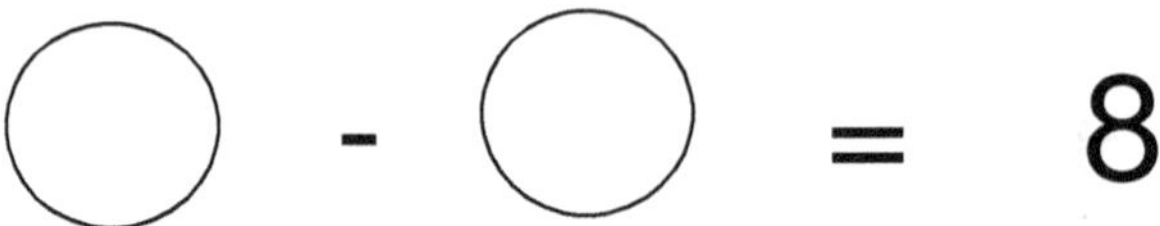

"So, they're not squares," said Tom deep in thought. "Red is eleven so we need three."

"Yellow!" said Shaun and punched the air. "Four less one is three!" They looked on the floor and quickly found the tiles they needed and slotted them in the brackets on the wall. Once again there was a 'ting' and the puzzle was bathed in green light.

"Two done! Next!" shouted Tom.

The five of them went to the next puzzle.

"Red square will be twelve," said Holly.

"And a blue diamond will give us five," Shaun blurted out enthusiastically.

"That leaves four," said Isabelle.

"That's a yellow square!" said Harvey.

"But wait!" Isabelle was standing with her hands on her hips. "A red diamond is eleven, a blue square is six and a yellow square is four. That will also give us twenty-one"

Holly was counting on her fingers.

"There's more than one combination. Which should we use?" Tom scratched his head.

"I don't know." Isabelle could feel her earlier panic returning.

"Let's just pick one and use it." Shaun was already looking for tiles. "Whichever combination we find first."

"But what if you get caught in the cage again?" said Tom.

"I think that if the answer is correct I should be fine. I'll take the chance. Let's find the shapes." Shaun clapped to spur the others on.

"But you'll get ten minutes this time if you're wrong." Holly looked up from searching the floor.

"I'll risk it!" said Shaun.

Yellow square, red diamond and a blue square was the first combination they found.

Shaun took the tiles and confidently slotted the first two in the brackets, but he looked a little nervous and hesitated before placing the third. He held his breath and slid the third tile in. There was a 'ting' and a green light and Shaun breathed a massive sigh of relief.

"Awesome!" called Tom. But he was beginning to worry about the amount of time they were taking. There were still seventeen sums to go.

Harvey must have been thinking the same thing. "I think we all know how this works now. Let's take one each and get through the rest of these quickly."

"Yes," Tom agreed, "and if anyone gets stuck, then just let the others know."

Shaun took the fourth puzzle and Harvey the fifth, Holly took puzzle six, Tom took the seventh, and finally Isabelle took puzzle eight. The sums were getting progressively harder as they moved further along the wall of the carriage towards the door that would take them into carriage three.

It wasn't long before Shaun, Harvey and Isabelle were scrambling along the floor looking for their pieces. Holly was still staring at her puzzle, counting on her fingers.

Tom looked at his puzzle with his hands on his hips:

$$\square \ + \ \square \ + \ \square \ + \ \square \ - \ 27 \ = \ -5$$

Minus five, thought Tom, take away twenty-seven to leave minus five, means that the shapes must total twenty-two. Blue is six, so three blue squares are eighteen, which leaves four. It must be a yellow square. Yes, that's it!

As he turned away to search for his puzzle pieces, he noticed Shaun had completed his puzzle with a 'ting' and a green light.

"Yeeessss!" Shaun exclaimed as he jumped in the air.

Isabelle was looking for pieces and Harvey had completed his puzzle and gave Shaun a high five as they moved on to the final two puzzles on the left wall. Holly had put some pieces in but was standing back scratching her head, looking confused.

Tom walked to the middle of the carriage looking down for his pieces. He quickly found three blue squares, but the only yellow square he could find was under Holly's foot.

He bent down to get it but it wouldn't move.

"Sorry, Holly, I need to get this piece." He tapped Holly on the shin.

"Oh, sorry, Tom. I think I've messed this up." She lifted her foot and Tom grabbed the yellow square off the floor.

"OK, don't panic, Holly, let's have a quick look." Tom looked at her puzzle and the piece she was holding in her hand.

"Yes, I see you've got two too many. Put the blue star down and use a yellow star instead."

"Thanks, Tom." Holly tossed the blue star away and went looking for a yellow star.

"You're welcome." Tom was happy he could help. He saw Isabelle complete her puzzle, and rush across the carriage to start the first puzzle on the right wall. He slid his tiles into his puzzle and he also received the 'ting' and green light. He had never been so happy to see a green light.

Holly had found her yellow star and was also greeted with a 'ting'. They headed to the right wall.

"I'm stuck. I don't understand this. Help, guys!" cried Isabelle from the first sum on the right wall.

"But you're usually so good at math," Tom frowned as he and Holly looked at Isabelle's sum.

$$\square + \square = 26$$

"I just don't understand it." Isabelle stamped her foot, frustration turning to desperation. Shaun and Harvey joined them and the five puzzleteers stared at the sum.

"How can that be? Square and square making twenty-six! The highest value color is red and that's twelve. Twelve and twelve is twenty-four. This doesn't make any sense!"

"Do you think they have made a mistake?" Harvey shrugged.

"No, the Conductor doesn't make mistakes," said Tom.

"Let's check the next one," suggested Shaun. "Maybe that will make more sense."

"The most we can make is twelve plus eleven which is twenty-three!" Isabelle's voice was becoming higher pitched.

"Are there any hidden spaces, or anything secret in the puzzle?" suggested Holly.

They checked the puzzle, pushing all around it and pulling at the brackets where the shapes fitted to try and find something hidden, without success. Shaun even he tried shouting at the sum. That didn't help.

"There's nothing secretive about the puzzles. Maybe we can put two tiles in one slot?" Harvey grabbed a blue pentagon and a yellow circle from the floor at random. He tried to put them both into one bracket at the same time but one tile slotted in and the other tile clattered to the floor.

"Wait!" said Tom, "blue and yellow together – that's it! – Five and three is eight. If they were squares that would be ten," he said excitedly.

"Yes, but we can't put two tiles in the same slot," protested Isabelle.

"No, but we can put a green square in the slot. Blue and yellow make green, six and four is ten! Remember that green square we found when we first came in here!"

"But we need twenty-six! We still need sixteen. That's a red plus a yellow," Isabelle said, still frustrated.

"Red and yellow make orange!" said Holly excitedly. "Are there any orange squares?"

They looked around and soon found the tiles. Tom took them and slotted them in straight in, receiving a 'ting' and a green light as a reward.

"Weren't you worried about getting a cage?" asked Isabelle.

"Yeah, but this is taking forever. We need to get a move on," replied Tom.

"What other colors can we make, Hols?" said Shaun.

"Umm, blue and red make purple. That will give us six plus twelve, eighteen for a square. And then I suppose seventeen for a non-square."

"Do we deduct two for a non-square? There are two colors after all," asked Harvey.

There was silence as the others contemplated this, until Tom spoke with authority.

"No, we only deduct one. The clue is always in the poem and the poem said, 'deduct one for a non-square'."

"Agreed. So an orange square is sixteen, other orange shapes are fifteen. Green is ten for a square and nine for the others." Holly summed up the other new colors.

"Brilliant! Well done, Hols. OK, great. We have nine puzzles left to go. Let's split up again and get them done as quickly as possible," said Tom.

They each went to a puzzle and started to work the sums out with their new knowledge. As for the left wall, the sums grew more difficult as they worked their way towards the door to the next carriage. Tom was looking at his puzzle, and was beginning to think he would need Isabelle's help.

$$\square \;+\; \square \;-\; \star \;+\; \square \;-\; 35 \;=\; 4$$

Phew! He thought this looked tricky, but then the voice of his gran came into his head.

"Don't worry. Do one thing at a time."

He took a deep breath. I need four and we're taking off thirty-five, which means the shapes add up to thirty-nine. I'll start with the star.

He started scanning the floor for a star, the first one he found was yellow and he decided to slot it in. He continued to think about the rest of the puzzle.

A yellow star is three so the squares add up to forty-two. Start with the high numbers. Purple is eighteen, so two of them will be thirty-six, that leaves me with six which is a blue square. Yes! He jumped up and punched the air with excitement.

He was off looking for the pieces he needed. He could see Harvey had already got his tiles and was going back to his puzzle, while Shaun was still looking for his. The two girls had the hardest puzzles and were still counting.

Tom grabbed two purple squares quickly. He went back to his puzzle and was slotting them into place when suddenly everything went dark, a red light flashed in the corner of the carriage and a deafening siren sounded. The lights went back on, the siren stopped, and Harvey was trapped in a cage. Tom could see a digital clock counting down from five minutes on the opposite wall between two of the completed puzzles.

The image of the Conductor appeared on the same wall. "Oh dear, Harvey, you will have to try harder at math when you get back to school!" He laughed and then he disappeared again.

Isabelle's puzzle went 'ting' and the green light came on. She went across to look at Harvey's puzzle.

"Oh, Harvey, you needed a green star, not a red star." She found a green star and replaced the red one. Another 'ting', another green light.

Tom managed to find his missing tiles and he also got a 'ting' and the green light, much to his relief.

"Sorry, guys, I just miscalculated," Harvey said from his cage.

"At least you only got five minutes," said Holly.

"You had better get on, there're still three puzzles left to solve and it looks like Shaun needs some help," Harvey pointed through the bars of his cage.

"Yes, please, guys. This is doing my head in!"

"Listen," announced Shaun. "You guys figure out what tiles we need and I'll go and find them. Maths is not my strong point."

"Good idea, Shaun," said Tom.

Holly and Isabelle calculated the sums and called out the tiles. Tom and Shaun went to find them and soon they were on the twentieth and last puzzle. It was the longest and hardest.

$$\square + \square + \square + \square - \bigstar - \Diamond + \triangle - \bigcirc = 18$$

Isabelle stood in front of it counting on her fingers and muttering numbers for nearly two minutes before declaring:

"We need a purple square, a blue square, an orange diamond, two yellow squares, a green triangle, a blue star and a yellow circle."

Shaun, Tom, Isabelle and Holly went off to find the tiles. By now the floor was a mess as they had walked over and searched through the tiles. Some were piled on top of each other, others were upside down and so were plain white and some had been kicked into the corners of the carriage.

"I've got a yellow," called Shaun from the middle of the carriage.

"Orange diamond here," Tom held the tile high and then passed it to Isabelle.

"Purple squares, blue star and the green triangle," Shaun called from the far corner.

"I've got the others except for a blue square," Isabelle slotted the tiles in.

Harvey urged them on from his cage as they searched for the elusive blue square.

Once the timer had ticked down to zero, Harvey was released from his cage and joined the search.

"I've looked all over this carriage floor about three times and they're definitely no blue squares left," said Shaun.

"What are we going to do?" said a wide-eyed Holly.

Tom looked at the completed sums. He saw the third puzzle and remembered the discussion they had.

"There's a blue square," he said pointing to the puzzle. "Do you remember we worked out there are different combinations that make twenty-one?"

"Yes, of course, I remember. A red square, a yellow square and a blue diamond will also give us twenty-one," said Isabelle.

Tom took the three tiles out of their slots and the green light disappeared.

"Here, Issy, here's your blue square. Quick, guys, can you find a red square, a blue diamond and a yellow square?"

Isabelle rushed off to the last puzzle and put the blue square in. There was a 'ting' and the green light appeared above the puzzle.

Shaun, Holly and Harvey quickly found the pieces Tom had asked for. They put them in place. 'Ting'. All twenty puzzles were now bathed in green light and the door at the end of the carriage opened automatically. The five puzzleteers rushed towards carriage three.

Can you help the puzzleteers to find which color tiles they will need to solve these puzzles?

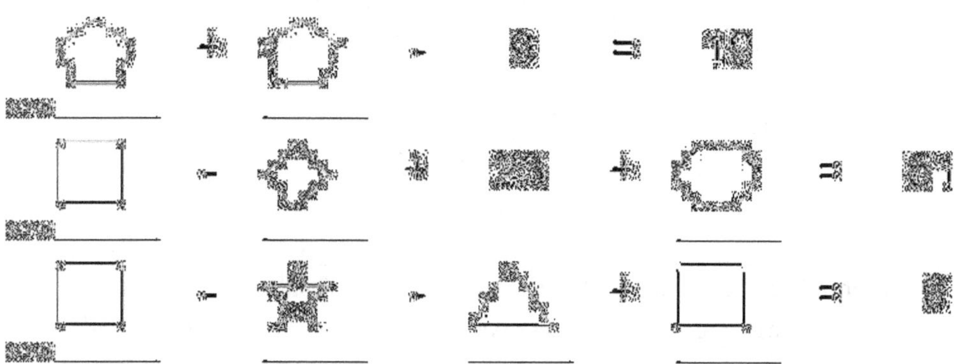

Chapter 13 - Pipes

Carriage three, my oh my,
Time has gone flying by.
Pipes and pipes and pipes some more,
Bring down the balls, not on the floor.
Work hard as a team. Hurry! Race!
Her place, his place, dat place, dis place.

Time remaining 57:24.
Thinking time remaining 01:00

Tom winced as he looked at the main clock. We spent a lot of time in that carriage, he thought, we're now three minutes behind schedule.

"That's a lot of places," said Isabelle.

"Maybe we have to find places for things." Harvey shrugged.

"Pipes and balls, what is it talking about?" said Shaun. "I don't understand."

"Neither do I." Holly shook her head. "This is the most confusing clue so far."

"We can't have the balls hitting the floor, but I still don't know what we will have to do," said Tom. "I've seen this kind of clue before, it'll make sense once we get in the carriage."

The minute ticked down, the door slid open and the puzzleteers rushed in. Another minute gone, only fifty-six to go. Just under an hour left on the Puzzle Train. Tom told himself to focus.

On either side of them there were clear pipes of every different length lying on the floor. The pipes were all straight and had a diameter about the same size as a golf ball.

"They're plastic," Shaun noted as he picked up two pipes and was banging them together.

He then tried to slot one pipe inside the other. 'Clack, clack, clack,' they went. It was no use. They wouldn't fit together. He threw them on the ground where they clattered onto the other pipes.

Harvey ventured further into the carriage where there was another pile of parts on the floor to the left.

"Look what we have here," he said. On the ground there lay more pipes, but some of these were shaped like an 'r' and some of them were shaped like a 'T'. He picked up one of the pipes that looked like an 'r' and showed it to the rest of the puzzleteers.

"This is a ninety-degree bend." He put it back and picked up one of the pipes that looked like a 'T'.

"This is a T junction. And look at this. There's a switch on it."
He clicked the switch backwards and forwards. Then he looked
inside the 'T' junction pipe and flicked the switch again.

"Look, when I move the switch, it moves this bit of plastic
inside, to the left." He clicked the switch. "Or to the right." He
moved the switch back.

"Hey, Shaun, pass me one of those pipes," Harvey said,
growing more excited with each new discovery. Shaun passed him
a small, straight pipe. Harvey pushed it into the 'T' junction pipe,
and put one of the ninety-degree bends on the other end.

"The pipes push into these like this!" He held up his handiwork
so the rest of the puzzleteers could see, feeling extremely proud of
himself.

"We have about a million plastic pipes and another hundred or
so 'r' and 'T' junctions. What do we do with them?" Tom was on
his knees inspecting the pipes.

"Guys, if you have finished playing around, take a look at this."
Holly was staring at the right wall of the carriage.

They swung round to look.

"Wow," was all Tom could manage.

"I can't believe I missed that!" said Harvey.

"You were too busy playing 'teacher' with the pipes," teased
Isabelle, smiling.

"The Conductor is a genius!" Toms eyes were as wide as
saucers.

At the top of the carriage wall, running from one end of the
carriage to the other, was a large clear plastic container. It was filled
with hundreds of silver ball bearings about the size of golf balls.
There were five downpipes from the container equally spaced along

its length. Each of these led down to a T junction, which branched off into a maze of pipes, looking like a plate of spaghetti as they wove around each other in all directions.

Some of the pipes led into a yellow circular junction around half way up the maze of pipes, about the size of a dinner plate. Stuck onto the front of this was a small label that read 'randomiser'.

"What's a randomiser?" asked Harvey. The puzzleteers stood for a moment and looked at the strange mechanism.

"The pipes run out at different angles," observed Holly.

"Well, I guess," said Isabelle thoughtfully, "that once something goes in, there's no way to tell which of the many pipes it will come out of." She rubbed her forehead. "Another one of the Conductor's little tricks."

"I guess we have to get the balls into this downpipe." Tom had walked to the maze and gave the middle pipe a tap with his knuckle. "There are seven pipes pointing at the floor, but this is the only one that doesn't point to the floor. The balls will go to this tank of water."

"Yes, look!" Holly spoke quickly. "The key's attached to this ball in this pipe poking up off the tank. It's floating. But I can't reach it." Holly pushed her fingers into the pipe, which stuck out from the tank at an angle.

Shaun tried to lift the lid of the water tank, but it was firmly fixed and would not budge. He kicked it in frustration, which made the water ripple a little but did nothing else.

"No wait," Tom told Shaun. "If you keep doing that you're going to get a cage again. We need to raise the water up the pipe until we can reach the ball."

"Of course! 'Dis place' from the poem. We need to displace the water. Well done, Tom," said Isabelle. "We just have to fill this container with something to bring the level of the water up."

"It must be those balls up there." Tom pointed at the container far above their heads.

Harvey was quiet while Tom and Isabelle were investigating the key. He was staring at the maze of pipes and tracing a path with his finger.

"This maze is incomplete. There're a lot of pipes missing."

"Of course, all the pipes that are on the floor," said Shaun.

"That's it!" said Isabelle. "We have to complete the maze and make sure the ball bearings from there," she pointed to the top container, "end up in the water tank."

"Yes, that's it. Clever Issy!" said Tom. "Harvey, you have been looking. Can you see where we need to put the pipes?"

"Yes, I'm pretty sure. Shaun, pass me a short pipe. Hols, pass me a ninety-degree bend."

"Harvey, you're a natural at this," said Tom.

"Ah, you see, my dad's a plumber. I must have picked up some of his talent." He inserted the pipe and the ninety-degree bend.

"Can you guys bring me some short pipes and some of the T junctions? I bet we have to connect every pipe, but I'm going to try to set up as many paths as possible leading to the water tank."

Harvey connected the first pipe easily. Then a 'T' junction and then tried four different pipes before he finally found one that fitted.

The next pipe took five attempts before he finally found the correct length. He wiped a drip of sweat off his nose.

"There are too many different pipes that are similar lengths. It's really hard to find the right one," he complained.

Harvey worked hard while the others helped by trying to find the right pipes.

"Grrr! Get in there, you stupid pipe!" Harvey yelled. The pipe was half a millimetre too wide and wouldn't connect into the 'r' junction. Eventually Harvey gave up and drop-kicked the pipe against the opposite wall, where it bounced off with a clatter and hit Isabelle on the back of her leg.

"Hey! That's not going to help complete the maze, is it?" She frowned at Harvey and rubbed the back of her leg.

"The stupid pipes aren't the same diameter! This is going to be impossible now!" Harvey kicked at a pile of pipes in frustration and sent them scattering all around the carriage.

"Enough now! Calm down!" Isabelle said sternly. The atmosphere in the carriage was getting tense.

"Take a break, Harvs," said Shaun.

"I don't need a break! I can do this!" Harvey looked to the ceiling and shook his fist. "The Conductor is sneaky."

"Shaun, come and help me sort these pipes by width," said Tom. "Issy, Hols, let's put the pipes we can't use in the corner. That will save us time."

"Sort the ones we can use by length as well," said Isabelle.

As a team, they quickly completed fitting the remaining pipes.

"What now?" Shaun looked at the maze of pipes.

"How do we release the balls from the container at the top?" Holly asked.

A hooter went off sound filled the carriage and the first ball dropped into the pipe at the far left.

"We need to use the 'T' junction switches to divert the balls through the correct pipes and into the middle here," Harvey spoke quickly.

Tom scanned the maze. There were dozens of 'T' junctions.

"Places quickly. Everyone take a section of the maze and get ready. Remember, direct the balls to the middle." Harvey directed the other puzzleteers. Tom took the centre of the maze with Shaun and Isabelle to his left and Holly and Harvey to his right.

The first ball dropped but not as quickly as anyone expected. When it hit a ninety-degree bend and rolled horizontally, it continued at the same speed.

"That's weird." Harvey frowned. "The ball should be moving way quicker than that."

"The Conductor has some advanced technology," said Isabelle. "I bet he has a vacuum or magnet system to control the balls."

The ball rolled across to the right. This was Shaun's side of the maze. He managed to adjust the necessary 'T' junctions and the ball rolled into Isabelle's area of the maze. She sent it through the middle pipe and into the water with a splash. The ball which held the key rose up very slightly in its pipe.

"Great start, guys, well done," said Harvey. Holly clapped and Shaun cheered.

The hooter sounded again. This time two balls were released from the top. One fell into the pipe on the far right and the other into the pipe in the middle. Harvey was on the far right and had to react quickly to divert the ball towards the middle.

Tom studied the ball that had dropped into the middle. He traced a path through the maze and watched with a growing smile on his face as the ball clicked and clacked its way through the maze and into the water. It was quickly followed by the ball from Harvey's side. The key rose up the tube slightly.

"Guys," said Tom, "now we have the switches set right, the balls will just run straight down into the water each time, won't they?"

"Yes, that makes sense to me," said Shaun.

The hooter went again. This time three balls were released into the pipes. They watched the progress of the balls. Two balls started following the same path. The leading ball reached a T junction and went right towards the water. As it passed through the T junction, the switch moved automatically so that the second ball went off to the left instead.

"N-o-o-o-o!" Tom realised instantly what happened. He frantically tried to change the switches to direct the ball back to the water but its path was inevitable, and it fell into the left-hand down pipe, thudding onto the carriage floor. The other two balls plopped into the water.

Tom's heart was in his mouth and everything seemed to happen in slow motion. The darkness… the siren… the red flashing light… and the cage was around Tom before he could even move.

The Conductor's silhouette appeared on the carriage wall and his deep booming voice filled the carriage. "Hahaha, three carriages and now three cages. Tom, do not underestimate me. Did you really think I would make it so easy for you? You were logical so you will only get five minutes, but everyone be warned. I will not be as generous next time."

The Conductor disappeared, replaced by a large red 5 which started to tick down.

Tom was always impressed at how the cages appeared as if from nowhere. He remembered reading an interview with the Conductor on the Puzzle Train website about the cages. All the Conductor would say was that it was an advanced technology that had taken years to perfect. There was never any chance to avoid them and they were completely immovable.

The cage was exactly the right height for him. If he stood on his toes his head brushed against the top. There was just enough space for him to turn around and the gap between the bars was just big enough for him to put his forearm through, but he was unable to reach any of the switches. The bars were cold to the touch and, try as he might, he couldn't move them one millimeter. He pushed the cage with all his strength, but it wouldn't move. He felt silly for underestimating the Conductor; it was a mistake he vowed to himself he would not make again.

Tom looked on helplessly from his cage, as the remaining four puzzleteers waited anxiously for the next release of balls. The seconds seemed to drag but then the hooter sounded again, releasing four balls into the maze.

"Take a ball each," instructed Harvey.

Learning from Tom's mistake, they tracked the balls through the maze. They bumped into each other as they switched positions and for a few seconds there was chaos.

"Oh no!" Holly covered her eyes as her ball entered the 'randomiser'.

All the other balls stopped dead where they were and for a second the chaos was replaced with an uneasy calm.

"What's going to happen?" asked Shaun. No one knew.

The 'randomiser' began to spin, accompanied by a low whistle. It spun slowly at first, then gained speed until the red writing was a blur, with a noise that reminded Tom of the washing machine at home when it was on its spin cycle. The noise grew louder for a few seconds and then the 'randomiser' stopped abruptly, went quiet, and Holly's ball shot out at great speed to the left, where it clattered back through the pipes and before anyone could react to change its path, it crashed into the clear plastic container at the top. As it stopped, the other balls started moving again.

"Whoa! That was cool!" exclaimed Harvey, as he flicked a switch and sent his ball to the water.

"That could have gone anywhere! Now it's right back at the beginning again," complained Holly.

Shaun was following his ball. It shot off to the right past where Isabelle was standing and went through a T junction. Shaun pushed past Isabelle in his eagerness to follow the ball.

"Hey, be careful," snapped Isabelle. "I almost lost my ball!"

"Sorry, Issy. Did it change that junction?" said Shaun.

"How should I know?" Isabelle retorted.

"Tom, trace the path of Shaun's ball and see if you can work out whether it changed the junction. Don't take your eyes off the balls, the rest of you," Harvey said with a large grin on his face. "This is a great puzzle!"

Tom was pleased to have something to do in the cage. Before Harvey had spoken, he spent his time between watching the time tick down very slowly and watching his friends operate the maze, desperate to get out and help. Tom traced the path of the ball and could see the switch had changed direction. He would tell Shaun when he had finished following his ball to the water tank.

Two balls splashed into the water. Holly diverted her ball so it wouldn't go through the 'randomiser' again and it plopped into the water a few seconds later. Isabelle checked the key. It was moving steadily up the tube but she still couldn't reach it with her fingers.

"We still need a few more, maybe eight or ten," she told Harvey.

"Shaun, you do need to change the T junction," Tom pointed at the junction as much as the cage would allow.

"Thanks, Tom," Shaun clicked the switch.

The hooter sounded again. This time, the blast was twice as long as the one before. One ball dropped into the middle pipe. The puzzleteers were confused.

"I'll take that," said Harvey. He had hardly finished speaking when a second ball was released from the pipe next to it.

"I've got that one," called Isabelle.

Another ball was released ten seconds after that then another ten seconds later. Soon the four of them were busy changing switches and following their balls through the maze. Fifth and sixth balls followed.

"Come on!" Tom urged both the puzzleteers and the clock. Harvey directed his ball into the water, but there were still five balls in the maze, and a sixth dropping from the top container. Three of the balls were being tracked by the puzzleteers. Harvey quickly found the fourth and started changing switches, but the other two were following a random course through the maze. Isabelle's ball splashed into the water and she scanned the maze frantically, looking for a ball.

At the top, another ball was released.

Isabelle spied the runaway and jumped to change a switch, but she was too late. The ball entered the 'randomiser'. Again, all the balls stopped as the 'randomiser' whirred, spinning faster and faster.

"Quick, check where the balls are while they're stationary." called Harvey.

There was a ping as the 'randomiser' stopped and threw the ball off at high speed diagonally to the right. It crashed into a stationary ball and both balls went spinning through the maze back up towards the top. The three remaining balls continued on their paths again and yet another ball was released from the top.

Tom turned to look across the carriage at the clock. He had only a few seconds left. He looked back at the maze and could see the four children absorbed with following their balls through the maze.

But wait! There was an unattended ball trickling towards the bottom of the maze. Tom could see the ball was going to land on the floor unless the junction was changed. Tom willed the seconds away.

"Come on, come on!"

The cage disappeared into the ceiling. Tom leapt towards the switch and flicked it to the left just as the ball got there. He let out a sigh of relief as he realised he had managed to change it in time and the ball swung to the left. Harvey bumped into him, unaware he had been released from the cage, and Tom fell to the floor. Fortunately, Harvey was still able to concentrate on both his balls despite the bump. He was working rapidly to change the junctions as the balls progressed their way through the maze.

Three more balls splashed into the water in quick succession. The balls continued to drop from the top at ten second intervals.

"Welcome back, Tom," said Harvey. "It's much easier with five."

Splash, splash, two more balls dropped into the water and Isabelle dived towards the upright pipe. At last she was able to get her fingers around the float attached to the key and pulled it out. As soon as she did so, all the remaining balls in the maze stopped.

"Let's get out of here." Isabelle ran towards the carriage door, jumping over discarded pipes, put the key into the lock, turned it and pulled the door open.

Solve the puzzle to work out how many balls will be needed to raise the water in the tank, so Isabelle can retrieve the key:

How many ball bearings will Isabelle need?
To raise the water and get the key freed.
A twenty-litre tank is half full,
Raise by half to release the floating ball.
Seventy-five milliliters each ball makes,
How many balls will it take?

Chapter 14 – Knights and Bikes

Door four on the verge of the puzzle within.
Don't get trapped. The Conductor will grin.
Dot, dash, dot dot dash, the code of Morse,
How many times will you move the horse?
Cycle, but only as far as you must.
Shorter or further will be a bust.

Time remaining 45:17.
Thinking time remaining 01:00

Wow, half way through, Tom thought. Forty-five minutes had flown past but they were right on schedule. He had seen many adult teams struggle to get so far. We're doing well but we mustn't be complacent.

"Does anyone know Morse code?" Isabelle's voice was significantly higher pitched than usual.

"Never heard of it," said Shaun.

"Each letter has a series of dots and dashes, but I don't know what they are."

"Sounds stupid." Shaun waved his hand dismissing the idea.

"It's not stupid, just old-fashioned." Isabelle frowned at him.

"I'm sure the Conductor won't expect us to know Morse Code, Issy." Tom put his hand on her arm to calm her down.

"What about horses and cycling?" Holly pointed at the poem. "It's confusing."

"I still don't know about Morse code," Isabelle whispered to Tom.

"Me neither," admitted Tom. "Try not to panic. That's what the Conductor's after. It's a trick he uses often."

The door slid open and they rushed in.

"What is this? A massive chess board?" Isabelle looked at the floor, the first three quarters of which consisted entirely of black and white squares set out in a chess board pattern. The squares were about twenty centimetres in size.

"Don't touch them yet, Shaun," called Tom as Shaun had walked to the center of the black white squares to inspect three large chess pieces.

"What are they?" wondered Harvey aloud, looking at the chess pieces.

"They're white knights," answered Isabelle. The three knights came up to Isabelle's knee. "That must explain the horses in the poem."

Tom walked towards the end of the carriage. He glanced at the chess pieces as he walked past but he was curious about three objects fixed to the floor at the end of the carriage. The chess board pattern ended, the floor here was plain blue.

"They're just exercise bikes," Tom called, a hint of disappointment in his voice. "Nothing unusual. Although it does explain cycling from the poem. Well, sort of." He inspected them carefully. They seemed perfectly normal. They weren't connected to anything else.

"I've never played chess. I don't know how. What do we do with these pieces?" Shaun gestured to the knights.

"In chess, a knight moves two squares forward and one to the side," said Isabelle.

"Or one forward and two to the side," added Holly.

"Or they can go backwards," said Harvey.

"They're right in the middle. We don't even know which direction we must move them!" Isabelle couldn't keep the desperation from her voice.

"Three knights, three exercise bikes and five of us. I don't get it," said Tom.

He walked back from the bikes and joined the rest of the puzzleteers who were standing around the chess pieces.

"We're missing something," agreed Harvey.

"What did the poem say?" said Tom. "There's always a clue in the poem."

Shaun rolled his eyes, thrust his hands in his pockets and ambled over to one of the exercise bikes and started kicking the wheel at the front.

"What's up with you?" Harvey glared at Shaun.

"Nothing," Shaun snorted and stared at the carriage wall muttering about football.

"Why don't you help, instead of sulking?" Harvey snapped.

Tom had seen this happen on the Puzzle Train many times. Teams would get stuck on a clue and in the confined space of the carriage they would start arguing. Usually that would mean they wouldn't get any further.

"Harvey, Shaun, we need to work together; otherwise we won't get out of here." Tom's tone was firm.

"So what?" said Shaun. "This is just stupid! I've had enough now."

"Do you want to spend the next forty minutes in here just waiting for the end of the show or do you want to help us?" Tom demanded, frowning. Shaun looked at the floor. Tom raised his eyebrows and his tone softened.

"Come on, Shaun. I'm sure you don't give up on the football pitch. Don't give up now. The clue is always in the poem."

There was an awkward silence as the five children looked around at each other.

"All right," Shaun mumbled. "Let's not give up on this, let's give it our best shot." A hint of a smile formed on his lips.

Harvey narrowed his eyes and looked at Shaun for a few seconds then shrugged his shoulders and brushed his hair out of his face.

"Back to the poem then,"

"Don't get trapped, for a start," blurted Holly.

"Then something about Morse code, but I don't see anything here that has anything to do with Morse code," said Isabelle. "We have found the horses and the bikes but I don't know how many times we have to move them or how far we have to cycle."

They looked around the rest of the carriage. The lighting in the carriage was bright and they could see every corner clearly. Except for the chess pieces and the exercise bikes there was nothing else. No other clues. The five of them stood in the middle looking utterly confused, trying to find anything that would help them.

Tom had seen groups of puzzleteers standing around on the Puzzle Train before as well. Often, they would become frustrated and do something rash and get caught in a cage. Tom could imagine if he was at home watching this on TV. Marvin would come into the picture now and remind everyone at home that it was a race against the clock and the puzzleteers would need to do something soon.

He could also imagine Marvin coming up with a cheesy joke to entertain the viewers at home. There are chess pieces so he would probably say something like the Conductor had them in checkmate.

Or maybe he would refer to Morse code and say they needed to dash. Wait, maybe that was it. Perhaps they should try dashing. Was that the clue?

"Let's check the walls for hidden panels," Harvey exhaled loudly. "Come on, Tom. Tom, wake up, let's go!"

Tom stopped imagining Marvin making cheesy jokes, ignored Harvey and ran towards the door they came in from. He then ran into the left-hand corner of the carriage, swung around and ran into the other corner.

"Tom, what are you doing?" said Isabelle.

"Dashing," said Tom. "Morse code is dots and dashes. I thought I would try dashing."

"Worth a try, I suppose," Isabelle nodded.

Isabelle, Harvey and Holly checked the carriage sides for hidden panels and Shaun inspected the exercise bikes, although he quickly became frustrated and started kicking the front wheel again.

Tom dashed from the right-hand corner all the way to the front of the carriage. He dashed so quickly that he had to put his hands out in front of him to stop from bumping into the front wall. He dashed to the other front corner of the train.

Isabelle was looking at the wall, rubbing her hands on it to try and find a hidden panel or a switch. She stepped onto a black square to her left and it gave a beep, similar to a car horn, which made her jump.

Isabelle jumped off the square. "Did you hear that?"

She put her foot back on the square, and again, it beeped.

"Remember that square, Issy," panted Tom from the front of the carriage. He was getting out of breath.

"You're not fit," Shaun pointed out.

"Tread on all the squares. Let's see what they do."

All five of them started treading on squares. Most of them did nothing but Shaun found another square that made a beep. Harvey found a square that made a longer beep.

"We need a way to remember where the squares are. That'll save us time!" said Shaun.

"That's a good idea, but how? There're hundreds of squares!" Harvey stood on his square again, just to make it beep.

"We could take a shoe off and leave it on the square," suggested Holly.

"Cool, good idea." Shaun took one shoe off, left it on the square and then walked in a very lopsided manner around the carriage looking for other beeping squares.

Tom and Harvey also took a shoe off to mark their squares and starting limping around.

They trod all over the chess board, being careful not to disturb the three knights in the middle. They discovered three squares that made short beeps and two that made slightly longer sounds.

"Great! Five squares, five of us, what next?" said Shaun.

"I'm putting my shoe back on first," laughed Harvey.

"Let's try standing on them all at the same time," suggested Holly.

"Cool! Everyone, stand by a square," said Harvey.

They took their positions. Tom looked at the other four puzzleteers, they were all standing around the edge of the carriage.

"That was it," Tom slapped himself on the forehead. "From the poem, we ignored the first line where it said on the verge. Verge means edge, we're all on the edge."

"Clever, Tom. About ten minutes too late, but still clever." Shaun winked at Tom, the jibe was good natured.

"On three. One. Two. Three," called Harvey.

They all stepped on their squares at the same time. There were five beeps but nothing else happened.

"Let's try going one by one," suggested Tom.

"Who goes first?" asked Holly.

Tom considered this for a moment, then said, "We'll go clockwise. Shaun, you start. You're closest to where twelve would be if the carriage was a clock."

Shaun stepped on his square. 'Beep'. Followed by the others. They looked around and again nothing happened.

"I've had enough of this." Shaun stamped his foot on his square. "It's stupid."

"Stop complaining and being a pain and try to help!" Isabelle almost screamed at him.

Tom could feel the tension building again and spoke quickly to try and calm the situation

"No. It's not, Shaun. It's logical. It's always logical. When you have seen the show enough times like I have, you know the Conductor has already given us the clue. We just need to find it," Tom explained patiently.

"But what is it, Tom? What are we missing?" asked Holly.

Tom took a deep breath and thought back to his gran and the times they used to watch the Puzzle Train together at her house.

"Oh, I like the Conductor," she would say. "He always gives so many clues in the poem."

The poem, Tom thought. "Hey, Issy, what did the poem say about Morse code?"

"Umm, dot, dash, dot dot dash, the code of Morse."

She's got such a good memory, thought Tom. Often teams would forget the poem and that's when they really struggled.

"I think the longer beeps are dashes. Let's try copying the order from the poem."

"Worth a try," said Harvey.

"Shaun, you go first on count of three, then Holly, then you, Issy, Harvey and finally me. One, two, three and Shaun …"

Beep, beeep, beep, beep, beeep. There was a small triumphant fanfare and a secret panel emerged from the wall on the left of the carriage. They rushed to inspect it:

Morse code: A-M
A dot dash
B dash dot dot dot
C dash dot dash dot
D dash dot dot
E dot
F dot dot dash dot
G dash dash dot
H dot dot dot dot
I dot dot
J dot dash dash dash
K dash dot dash
L dot dash dot dot
M dash dash

"Wow, I had no idea what Morse code even was," said Shaun.

There were supposed to be six of us. Could the Conductor have changed the puzzle while we were moving, wondered Tom, full of admiration. His thoughts turned briefly to George. I hope he's all right. Then the image of the ticking clock focused his attention back to the puzzle.

"That's great, but where's the rest of it? And what do we do with it now we have it?" asked Harvey.

"There're three chess pieces and three exercise bikes. Maybe we have to do it three times," said Shaun.

"Yes, I like it! Well done, Shaun," said Tom excitedly. "Quick, let's get back to our squares and do it again as fast as we can." Tom sounded anxious. They had wasted a long time doing nothing in this carriage.

They hurried back to their squares and repeated the pattern. They were greeted with a second fanfare and a second secret panel was revealed next to the first one. They ran over and inspected the second panel.

Morse code: N-Z
'N dash dot
O dash dash dash
P dot dash dash dot
Q dash dash dot dash
R dot dash dot
S dot dot dot
T dash
U dot dot dash
V dot dot dot dash
W dot dash dash
X dash dot dot dash
Y dash dot dash dash
Z dash dash dot dot'

"Quick, once more, and let's see what happens," said Tom.

They rushed back to their squares again and completed the sequence for a third time. Another secret panel opened in the opposite wall to the Morse code panels.

They hurried over to look at the new panel. A marker pen dropped from the ceiling when they reached it. Shaun picked it up. The panel was large enough for the five of them to stand around and see this new part of the puzzle. At the top were three patterns of dots and dashes, and underneath each pattern were two rows of boxes.

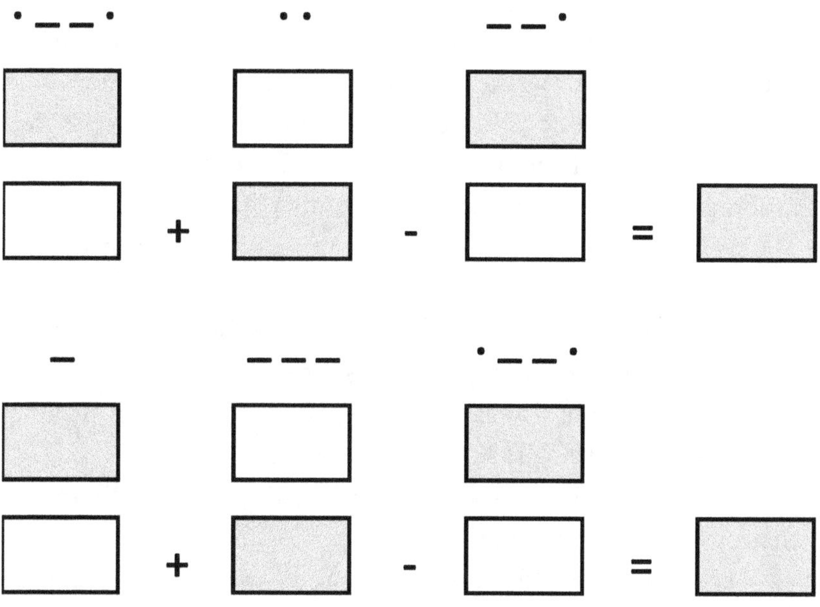

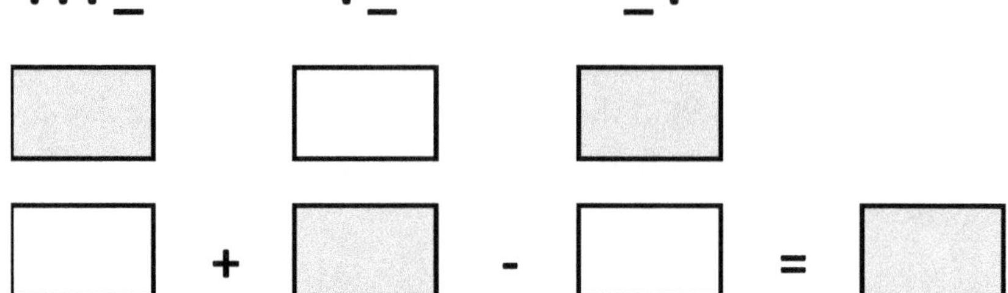

They all looked at the panel trying to decide what they needed to do next. Isabelle was the first to comment.

"It's Morse Code. We need to get the letters and write them into the top rows. Then the bottom row of boxes seems to be a sum, so somehow we need to work out a number."

"What do we do with the number then?" Shaun frowned and folded his arms.

"The poem said we need to move the horse a number of moves!" Tom said clapping his hands together.

"But the poem also said we have to cycle a certain distance. Maybe it's that." Isabelle scratched her head.

The five puzzleteers stood around looking at each other for an answer which didn't come.

"We'll work out the puzzle and then worry about what the number is for." Tom took control of the situation. He started walking to the left of the carriage where the Morse code panels were.

"What have we got first?" he called over his shoulder.

Harvey called across the combination of dots and dashes while Tom looked them up on the table

"That's a 'P'," Tom called back across the carriage. Isabelle wrote 'P' down in the first box. "Then 'I', then 'G'."

"PIG! But how do we make that into a number?" said Holly.

"The only thing I can think of is that each letter has a corresponding position in the alphabet." Isabelle counted on her fingers. "That would make 'P' sixteen, 'I' nine, and 'G' seven." She wrote down the numbers. "Then the sum. Sixteen plus nine minus seven is eighteen. We have to move the first one eighteen times."

Shaun ambled over the carriage to join Tom. Isabelle called out the second series of dots and dashes and Tom let Shaun reply with the letters. This spelt the word 'TOP', which Isabelle quickly worked out was nineteen.

The third and final series of dots and dashes spelt 'VAN' which Isabelle calculated was nine. She wrote all the numbers on the board.

"So that's, eighteen, nineteen and nine. Is it horses or cycles?" said Isabelle.

"Wait, I know!" said Harvey puffing his chest out. "Look at the box pattern. It has to be the knights!"

The others looked from the wall to the floor and back to the wall.

"How do you work that one out, Harvey?" asked Shaun.

"Well look, the box pattern is a white box, then a grey box, alternating... do you see?" He waved his hand at the grid on the wall.

"Yeah, but they're grey boxes on the wall. On the floor they're black," pointed out Holly.

"That's the clever part. The chess pieces are white but they're on black squares. Black and white together make grey." Harvey was very pleased with himself. "What d'you think?"

"I think you're nuts," smiled Shaun, "but I think this Conductor is equally nuts, so I agree." He chuckled. "Which one do we start with?"

"The one on the left. The first panel opened on the left," said Holly and without waiting for a reply she picked up the knight on the left. She was about to move it, but then doubt crept into her and she paused.

"But wait, which way do I move it?"

The five of them looked at each other. They had no idea.

"Let's move it forwards. Forwards is the way we want to go!" Shaun said positively.

"Sounds good to me, Shaun!" said Tom.

Shaun smiled. Tom's comment made him feel part of the team.

Holly picked up the left-hand knight and moved it two spaces forward and one to the left. A green light appeared inside the knight as she placed it down.

"How did you know to go left?" Isabelle said.

"I didn't, it just felt right.".

"You were lucky!" said Harvey.

"That green light has to be a good sign, Hols," said Shaun.

"I'll move it. You guys keep count," suggested Holly.

The others counted as Holly moved the knight, and each time it was placed down a green light appeared.

"That's only eleven, Hols," said Harvey,

"I've run out of space," and before anyone could say anything Holly counted one square back and two to the right and placed the knight down. The knight turned green and Holly breathed a sigh of relief.

"How did you know to do that!" Tom's voice was unusually high.

"Yeah. that was lucky, Hols!" Harvey puffed his cheeks out and blew his hair off his forehead.

"I didn't really think about it, I just moved it!" Her cheeks flushed pink. "But it all worked out well in the end."

On the eighteenth move, the knight turned completely green and three numbers became visible across its back.

"It says two, seven and three," called Holly.

"What are they for?" Harvey asked.

"Perhaps that's how far we have to cycle on the bikes," said Isabelle.

Shaun rushed over towards the bikes.

"That's it!" Tom cried. "Start with the one on the left."

"Will do!" Shaun jumped on the bike and started pedalling. The display came to life and started counting: 001. 002. 003'. The others stood and watched him.

"Someone go and move the next knight," Shaun called from the bike.

"Yeah, he's right," said Tom. "We need to get a move on."

Holly and Isabelle ran over to the knight.

"Issy, you keep count," said Holly.

"Nineteen moves this time, Hols."

The girls started moving and counting. The boys were watching Shaun on the bike. He was pedalling hard and a few beads of sweat were starting to appear on his forehead.

"Two hundred and fifty-five… two hundred and sixty-five… two hundred and seventy. Now slow down," Harvey called.

Shaun slowed and the display screen ticked over, two hundred and seventy-one, two, three.

"*STOP!*" called Harvey.

The screen showed two, seven, three. The exercise bike was covered in green light.

"Green again. That's good, yeah?" Shaun wiped his forehead on his sleeve but didn't seem to be out of breath at all.

"Definitely," Tom nodded.

Holly called over to the boys.

"Finished! Five, two, nine."

Shaun hopped straight on the second bike and started pedalling furiously.

Holly moved the third knight the nine times she needed to. Shaun was only half way through his pedalling. He was fit from all his football training, even so he began to puff as the display went over five hundred. The display ticked over to five, two, nine. Shaun was now sweating heavily and out of breath from his pedalling. He wiped his forehead on his sleeve again but the exercise bike was covered in a green light so he was very pleased with himself.

Holly called "Six, two, two."

Harvey hopped on the third bike and started pedalling. Shaun was relieved and panted a thank you. Harvey wasn't as fit as Shaun and started huffing and puffing after three hundred and struggled to get up to six, two, two but made it through sheer determination. He was panting and sweating and he stayed on the bike after it turned green to catch his breath.

All the bikes were now covered in green. As the third lit up, a key fell from the ceiling and landed next to the middle bike.

"Yes! Carriage four complete." Tom clenched his fists. Shaun and Harvey gave a high five, the earlier tension between them now lifted.

Shaun grabbed the key, put it in the lock, turned it and then pulled the handle towards him. He yelled a triumphant "Let's go!" as the door opened and they went through.

Knights move two squares in one direction and then one square at a ninety-degree angle to make a 'L' shape. What's the fewest moves you can make to land on the square with the exercise bike and then the square with the key?

Chapter 15 – Super Shots

Carriage five, don't get cross, join the dots.
'bet the order, power up your Super Shots.
Make all connections, no time to lose,
Hit the reds and not the blues.
Two chances only at this stage,
Otherwise you'll end up in a cage.

Time remaining 27:35
Thinking time remaining 01:00

Tom was aware that the others were discussing the clue, but he was worried. We spent twenty minutes in that last carriage, he thought to himself. We're now three minutes behind schedule again. On the plus side, we had no cages so we are all still together. We have to hurry through this one if we are to have time to even attempt the final carriage.

Tom was shaken out of his thoughts when Holly tapped him on the shoulder and asked, "What do you think?"

"Umm." Tom didn't stop to think. He just said, "I don't know what a Super Shot is but I'm pretty sure we have to work out an electrical connection to them to 'power them up'. The dots are probably where we need to put the cables."

"And 'bet the order'. What do you think that means? Will we have to place bets on something?" asked Isabelle.

"You mean gambling? No, definitely not. The Conductor won't put anything random in the puzzles. There's always order and logic," said Tom.

"There's an apostrophe before 'bet'," Isabelle began but was interrupted because the minute clock ticked down, the door slid open and the puzzleteers rushed into the carriage, the door sliding closed behind them automatically.

Down the middle of the carriage, running from front to back there were six chairs. Evenly spaced apart and facing the left wall. They were made of grey plastic, with footrests, armrests and a red harness above with each supported by a single silver stand.

"They look like the chairs from my hairdresser," commented Holly.

"Except the harness looks like something from a roller coaster," added Tom.

"Do you get your hair cut at a theme park?" laughed Harvey. Holly stuck her tongue out at him.

On the carriage wall to their left in the corner was a massive light switch. It was white and easily the biggest light switch Tom had even seen. It was nearly as tall as he was. The switch had the word 'OFF' in large letters above it and 'ON' underneath it. The switch was in the 'OFF' position.

Opposite the switch, attached to the right wall, were twelve thick, blue cables each with a silver connector at a ninety-degree angle at both ends. The longest stretched almost from the ceiling of the carriage to the floor. The cables were progressively shorter as they got closer to the other end of the carriage. The shortest was half the length of the longest.

"There's more wires here," called Holly as she walked along the right wall of the carriage. "Seven. All different colors."

Tom joined her. The wires were the thickness of Tom's phone charger cable and each one was around twelve inches long. There was yellow, blue, red, white, orange, black and green wires. Like the thick blue cables each had a connector at a ninety-degree angle at both ends.

"There's a cable running from the switch. It looks the same as those ones on the wall." Harvey was looking from the switch to the thick blue cables. "It disappears here into the floor through this brass circle."

"I think I see what's going on. Look there's more of those brass circles on the floor here." Tom came over to investigate. "And there's the same blue cable joined to this first chair."

"This is weird!" said Shaun looking around the carriage. "What do we do?"

"The clue is always in the poem," said Tom. "What have we got? Chairs in the middle and lots of cables."

"Join the dots!" exclaimed Holly. "These look like dots!" She tapped one of the brass circles with her foot.

"Brilliant, Hols," said Shaun as he walked towards the thick blue cables. "We must have to use these to join them up." Then something caught his eye further over on the wall of the carriage and he went to investigate.

Isabelle was counting. "We only need seven of them to join the dots. There are twelve cables."

"The Conductor doesn't make his puzzles easy, Issy. I bet the brass circle is a cap and we have to push these connectors into the floor," said Tom, holding the end of one of the blue cables.

Holly and Isabelle knelt to inspect the caps. Tom and Harvey joined them. After experimenting with pulling, pushing and trying to lever the caps off, they discovered they were able to twist them.

"They twist! Quick everyone, let's get them all off," Isabelle instructed.

Shaun tossed the cap he removed to the side casually where it clattered into the far wall.

"Be careful, young Shaun," the Conductor's voice echoed through the carriage. "I don't like a mess."

Shaun looked nervously to the ceiling, fearing a cage, but none came.

"Don't worry," Tom reassured him. "Let's get these cables now." Tom led the way to the wall and tried to pull a cable out of its clip.

"Gnnn," he grunted as he tugged harder. The cable disconnected from the top clip and flopped on Tom's shoulder.

"Phew! That's heavy!" He could only just wrap his hand around the cable, it was so thick. After going red in the face and a few hard tugs, the cable clicked away from the bottom clip.

The girls and Shaun were also busy trying to get the blue cables from the wall, but Harvey stood still, scratching his head.

"So we connect the thick blue cables to each connection in the floor?"

"Right, and then that forms the connection between the giant switch and the chair," said Tom.

"I get it," confirmed Harvey. "Then we turn the switch on. That powers the chairs. Then what?"

"That's what we have to find out," interrupted Holly. "I love this!"

Harvey still wasn't happy.

"What about these thin multi-colored wires?"

"I think they go in the wall over there." Shaun pointed to the far corner where he had been investigating.

Tom dropped the cable on the floor as they all rushed to the wall, where they could see small holes at intervals. There were single holes at the far left and right. In the middle the holes were in pairs and looked like figure eights.

"Yes, look." Tom crouched. "There's a connector on the floor here, right next to this smaller hole."

"Yes," exclaimed Harvey. "The electrical current runs across the floor to here, through the blue cables. Then it goes up the wall through the small wires." He traced the holes in the walls with his hand, "and back down to the floor over there, through more blue cables until it reaches the chairs."

There was a brief silence. Harvey began to doubt himself.

"Am I right?"

"You're right," laughed Holly.

"Let's stop standing around and get these wires connected." Shaun clapped them into action.

They unclipped the rest of the cables from the side of the carriage. The longest cable took both Shaun and Tom to carry it.

"Can't we just connect the switch straight to the chairs?" said Holly. "This cable is about the right length!"

"No, I'm sure we will have to use all the connections," said Tom. "The Conductor won't make it that easy for us."

"The poem did say *all* the connections," said Isabelle.

"Which order do we join the connections in?" asked Holly.

That's a good question, thought Tom.

"I don't know. We'll just have to try and see. Start at the switch." Tom could hear his gran's voice telling him to be logical.

"Put this cable by the switch and see if it reaches any of the dots." Shaun and Tom placed the cable down and moved it around the carriage to see if it would reach any of the connections. It didn't.

"Now try this one." Harvey had the next longest thick blue cable over his shoulder and dropped it to the ground with a grunt.

"That's heavy," he complained rubbing his shoulder.

"You boys try and get these floor cables sorted. Holly and I will connect up these multi-colored wires on the wall," said Isabelle.

Tom gave her a 'thumbs up' and the girls walked over to investigate the wall connections.

The three boys tried the cable, checking from the switch in all directions around the carriage floor. Again, the cable wouldn't reach a connection.

They grabbed the next longest thick blue cable from the wall and tried again. To their relief, it reached a connection along the left wall perfectly.

"That's great, it must be this one," said Harvey.

"We'd better check the rest just in case one wire reaches that further connection." Tom pointed to the other brass circles in the floor.

"That's going to take ages," complained Harvey.

"It will save us time in the long run," said Tom. "We'd better get a move on!"

"Great," Shaun panted after they checked the remaining cables. "Let's put this in and get the next one." Shaun pushed the wire into the connection.

"The clue is in the poem." Isabelle rubbed her chin as she contemplated the colored wires. "Those chairs must be the Super Shots somehow. We're joining the dots to get the power from the switch to the chairs."

"Right," agreed Holly. "'Don't get cross'. I guess that means that we shouldn't cross any wires."

"Agreed," nodded Isabelle. "Now, 'bet the order', that's the important part, I'm sure."

"Yes!" Holly jumped on the spot, "but how? What order do we put them in?"

"Yes, what is the order?" Isabelle considered. "We definitely have to use all the cables and they're all the same length. In the poem, the word 'bet' had an apostrophe before it."

"So?" said Holly.

"Well that means a word has been shortened. There are missing letters," Isabelle explained.

Holly was looking at the wall. "I think we should start from the left but..." She was interrupted by Isabelle.

"Alphabet!" Isabelle exclaimed. "'Bet the order – alphabetical order!"

"Yes, clever!" Holly agreed and they high-fived.

"I think we start from the left as well. We started from the left in the last carriage. it seems logical," said Isabelle.

"So blue first… no wait… black then blue." Holly handed them to Isabelle who put the first connector into the hole in the wall. Holly passed Isabelle the cables in order: green, orange, red, white and finally yellow, while Isabelle pushed them into the wall. As she was connecting the red wire, they heard raised voices. By the time she connected the yellow wire, there was a full-blown argument going on.

"Don't get cross," Isabelle quoted from the poem and smiled at Holly.

They turned from the corner of the carriage and could see four thick blue cables in place but Shaun and Harvey were arguing about the fifth wire. Tom was looking down at his shoes, thinking.

"Put this one in there!" Shaun was waving a cable, frowning and using it to gesture to a hole to his left.

"No! You can't do that. Look, because then the only way to connect the next cable is to go across that cable." Harvey was pointing; his face was red.

"What do you suggest then?" Shaun, an angry look on his face, stood toe to toe with Harvey, staring up at him.

Tom gathered his thoughts and took a breath. Usually he wouldn't get involved. He didn't like arguments, but this was the Puzzle Train. Any time it looked like a fight between puzzleteers, would mean cages. Be brave, he told himself.

"Cool it," he ordered as he stepped between them and portrayed a calm he didn't feel. It felt like his heart was thumping at twice its usual pace and was somehow located in his throat rather than his chest.

"Harvey's right. Sorry, Shaun, you can't do that. The poem said 'don't get cross'. It meant don't have any cables cross any others." His heart began to go back to normal.

Shaun threw his cable down and muttered something angrily. He began to turn away but stopped.

"But we've tried the other combinations. We can't get back to the final connection by the chair!"

"I've been trying to tell you, the fourth cable is wrong," Tom stood tall.

"No, it isn't!" Harvey was on the defensive. "I put that cable in."

"Look, Harvs," said Tom, clapping him on the shoulder. "Let's just try a different cable and see."

Shaun was only too happy to remove the cable that Harvey had connected incorrectly. Harvey didn't sulk for long, realising the importance of getting the puzzle completed quickly.

Holly and Isabelle came over to help the boys.

"We're finished with the colored wires."

"That's it!" called Harvey. "All the cables are in."

Holly ran over to the switch and moved it to the 'ON' position. She had to use both hands. The switch made a loud 'click'.

A siren blasted, but it was different from the one that meant a cage was about to drop. It was quieter, and sounded somehow happier. The carriage was plunged into darkness and the five children stood totally still.

"What's going on?" asked Shaun nervously.

After a second or two, the cable that led from the switch started to turn a luminous green. The green light flowed like water filling up a hosepipe as it made its way to the second cable. It flowed through all the floor cables, then up the wires in the wall, filling the carriage with a green glow. When the light hit the connection at the first chair a yellow light went on above it. One by one each chair was covered in the same yellow light, except for the chair nearest to the entrance to carriage six.

That would have been for George, thought Tom.

A deep robotic voice echoed through the carriage. "Take your seats in ten… nine…"

"Quick, everyone, get on the seats in the middle." Isabelle had to shout over the sound of the countdown.

"… seven… six… five…" the voice continued.

Tom ran to the middle chair jumping over the green cables on the floor. He sat down in the seat facing the left-hand carriage wall. The harness automatically came down over his head and rested on his shoulders. He put his arms on the arm- rests and discovered a button there he hadn't noticed before.

Running for chairs, Isabelle and Shaun bumped into each other with an "oooof", but sat down in the first two seats before the timer counted down. Harvey ran to the seat to Tom's right. Holly was the last to react and only the chair furthest from her was available. She ran from the switch, but tripped over one of the cables and landed on all fours on the carriage floor.

"Holly!" called Harvey. "Are you all right?"

"Fine." Holly sounded annoyed and started rubbing her knee.

"Quickly, get to the chair," Harvey implored.

"Three… two… one… BEGIN!" called the robotic voice.

Holly stood up and was about to walk to her chair when she stopped, stunned by what she saw appear and stood still, wide eyed with her mouth open.

Across the left-hand wall, at head height, a life size image of each child's face appeared, so each puzzleteer was looking at him or herself. Tom looked down the line of smiling images. Beneath each was a large green number five and below that, just above the floor, was an orange number two.

"Two chances, from the poem," Tom tried to look to his left and right to tell the others, but his movement was restricted by the harness.

"Two chances for what?" replied Isabelle. Tom didn't know, but he did know they were about to find out.

From above Tom's head there was a small whining noise like an electric motor starting up. He looked behind him as best he could and saw a tube, about the same size as the middle of a toilet roll, on a metal arm which moved slowly over his head and came to a rest in front of his right eye. He closed his left eye and looked through it. The tube magnified his face slightly and had a cross printed in the middle.

"It's a sight," called Shaun from the end nearest the switch. "These must be the Super Shots."

Shaun had also found the button on his arm rest and he pressed it. On the carriage wall in front of him there was an electronic explosion, right in the middle of the forehead of his image. He was bouncing up and down on the chair, giggling.

"That was right in the middle of the sight! I think we're going to have to shoot something!"

"Look!" Holly pointed behind the chairs. "Planes!"

The four of them craned their necks to see behind them as best they could. Holly dashed towards her Super Shot.

Digital pictures started emerging on the right wall of the carriage. They looked and sounded like mini jet planes. There were eight of them, six red and two blue, and they were all moving in a straight line but at different angles. Some of them were going straight up the wall, some were moving at an angle from left to right, and some from right to left.

The planes were bright compared to the relative gloom of the carriage which was still bathed in the eerie green light coming from the floor.

"This is awesome!" said Shaun, "it's like we're in a massive shooting gallery. I bet we have to shoot down the planes before they get to us."

"But they're behind us!" called Harvey trying to look over his shoulder.

This was a problem. The Super Shots were stationary and the four of them were facing the left side of the carriage.

The jet planes were climbing slowly up the wall behind them, accompanied by a rumbling sound from their engines.

"Holly, quickly! Sit down!" called Isabelle from her seat next to Shaun. Holly had stopped once again to watch the planes, but now she jumped into her chair. The harness came down and her sight appeared in front of her as the jet planes were now flying over their heads across the ceiling.

The robotic voice filled the carriage again. "RELEASE."

There was a loud metallic 'clunk'. Shaun was twisting his body to try to get a good look at the planes when suddenly his chair began to move on its stand.

"Hey, check it out! I'm moving!" called Shaun.

He twisted his body to the right and to the left and was able to complete a full circle. He arched his back and pushed his shoulders into the chair and was able to look directly at the ceiling. He leaned forward as far as he could but the chair wouldn't point at the floor because the footrests banged into the stand.

The children followed Shaun's lead, all the Super Shots moved in the same way. Isabelle tilted back to face the ceiling, pressed her button and fired. There was an electronic explosion on the ceiling but her shot was behind the plane.

The planes had crossed the ceiling and were now descending the left side of the carriage towards the digital images of the puzzleteers.

"We can't let them hit our pictures. Shoot them! Shoot the red ones only! It's from the poem," shouted Tom.

Shaun took careful aim and when the plane was just behind the centre of the cross in his sights, he pressed his button and the red plane exploded.

"Yes!" he exclaimed.

The green five beneath his image changed to four.

"Aim for the plane when it's just behind the centre of the cross in your sights. The shot takes a second to reach the wall," he called.

Isabelle fired but the explosion just missed a plane to the left. She pressed the button again, once, twice, but nothing happened. On the third attempt the plane exploded in front of her.

"Yeehah!!" she shouted. "There's a delay of about three seconds each time you fire." Her green number also changed to a four.

The remaining planes were creeping towards their pictures. Behind them, unseen by the puzzleteers, more planes were crawling up the right wall but moving slightly more rapidly than the first wave of planes.

"I can't make my chair move," cried Holly. There was panic in her voice.

"You have to twist your whole body," called Tom.

Harvey shot down a plane. Tom missed his shot but after waiting three seconds he lined the plane up just behind the middle circle of his target, fired and hit it.

The second wave of eight planes was already on the ceiling. A third wave of planes was released behind them.

One of the red planes was heading directly to Holly's picture. She was twisting her body frantically. She had managed to start the chair moving but she was twisting far too fast and couldn't control her Super Shot.

"No!" Holly covered her eyes as the plane crashed into her picture. Her face changed from a smile, to a look of pain, and then turned sad. A siren sounded and the orange number two at the bottom turned to a red number one.

Harvey was in the Super Shot next to Holly. He turned to look at her. She was spinning around and looking as if she was becoming dizzy.

"Hols, stop panicking. Just keep calm. Try to move slowly. Just stay still and let it come to a rest."

Holly relaxed and the Super Shot slowly came to a halt. She found herself staring at the carriage door, held in tight by her harness. She twisted her body and found herself staring at Harvey. She arched her back and found herself staring at the ceiling.

"This is going to take some more practice," she mumbled to herself.

"Harvey, look out!" called Tom. Harvey was too busy helping Holly and wasn't paying attention to the planes. Tom took a shot at a red plane heading directly to Harvey's picture but missed and it crashed into Harvey's image. He was now also down to one.

Shaun took a shot and another plane exploded.

"Yes! I love this game!" His green number was now down to three.

Two blue planes flew harmlessly past their images. Shaun twisted around to look at the right side of the carriage just in time to see another wave of planes being released, this time moving even faster.

"Yes!" Shaun exclaimed as he shot another plane.

Tom and Isabelle both shot down planes. Harvey also did but was still trying to help Holly, who was still struggling with her Super Shot. She was unable to control it well enough to line up a plane in her sights. She fired off a shot but it exploded far away from the nearest plane which was already on the left side of the carriage and heading quickly towards her picture, which had now changed to a very worried looking face.

"Harvey, help!" she screamed. Harvey turned quickly to help and fired. The plane exploded.

"Thank you!" she called.

Shaun was enjoying shooting planes and was quickly down to zero.

"Awesome!" he called out again. The harness didn't release so he continued lining up planes and shooting them.

"Shaun, let me get down to zero as well," Isabelle complained. "Stop shooting my planes."

"Calm down, Issy, you just need to be a better shot," Shaun teased. Isabelle glared at him for a second and then realised she had better get back to shooting the planes.

There were two planes heading towards Holly's image, one red and one blue. Holly was still in a panic.

"Help me, Harvey, there are two planes." She shot and missed. The three seconds reload time seemed to take forever.

"Don't hit the blue one," Harvey reminded her. He was so busy helping Holly he didn't notice a red plane heading towards his own image.

Harvey and Holly shot at the same time. Harvey hit the red plane, Holly hit the blue one. The green lines from the cables faded, the planes disappeared and the carriage went black. The siren sounded and the red light flashed. Holly's Super Shot went back to its starting position and wouldn't move. A cage dropped from the ceiling covering both Holly and the Super Shot.

The red number one under Holly's image was replaced with a red ten, which then ticked down to 9:59.

The Conductor's deep booming voice filled the carriage.

"Hahaha, I told you next time would be ten minutes."

"Oh no, Hols," said Harvey, "are you OK?"

The Conductor disappeared, the green cable lights came back on and the planes reappeared in the same places they had been before.

"Harvey, look out!" Holly called back at him. A red plane was nearly at his image. He turned quickly and shot. The explosion was just above the plane and Harvey could only watch as the plane crashed into his image. For the second time in less than ten seconds the lights went off, the siren sounded, and Harvey was also trapped in a cage.

"Hahaha, unlucky Harvey. That was very gallant of you, but you must pay attention!" boomed the Conductor.

"Oh no!" said Isabelle.

"Isabelle, look out!" Tom shot and missed and a red plane crashed into her image. Her orange number two turned to a red number one.

"Pay attention, guys. Let's finish off these planes."

They kept shooting and both Tom and Isabelle quickly joined Shaun on zero.

As soon as they were all on zero, the remaining planes disappeared and were replaced with just one larger, green plane, moving very fast. It looked a bit like a key.

Unlike the other planes, this did not move in a straight line. It was unpredictable, moving across both sides and the ceiling in loops, figures of eight and zig-zags.

"It's quick. Aim slightly further in front of it than you did for the red planes!" Shaun lined up the plane and shot. Success! He hit the plane and his Super Shot returned to its starting position and wouldn't move.

Tom and Isabelle were both following the plane with their Super Shots. Tom was beginning to find the movement hard work now. His sides were aching and he was getting out of breath. He fired and missed.

Isabelle fired and hit. Her Super Shot also returned to its starting position and wouldn't move.

Tom fired again and missed again.

"Come on, Tom, you can do it!" Shaun, Holly and Harvey all cheered him on.

He took a deep breath and followed the plane onto the ceiling and fired again. Hit! The plane digitally exploded and a plastic rectangle, the size of a bank card fell and hit the floor. Tom's Super Shot returned to the starting position and all three harnesses went up.

The carriage lights came on. The green lights of the cables went out and turned blue again. Isabelle picked the key card up. Holly and Harvey watched from their cages. Tom looked over to the left wall which told him they both had eight minutes left.

"Don't wait for us, you guys. Go on to the final carriage," said Holly.

"Yes, you must. We'll try and catch up if we can," agreed Harvey.

"Are you sure?" said Isabelle looking sad. "We have been through so much together."

"Yes, now go! Go and crack the final puzzle."

"Thank you, guys. We'll see you soon."

"Good luck!" called Harvey as Isabelle swiped the card in the reader. The door slid open. Holly and Harvey waved to Shaun, Tom and Isabelle as the three successful puzzleteers walked through to the final carriage, the door sliding shut behind them.

Can you connect the three switches to the three Super Shots below? Each switch must connect to each Super Shot without any of the lines crossing.

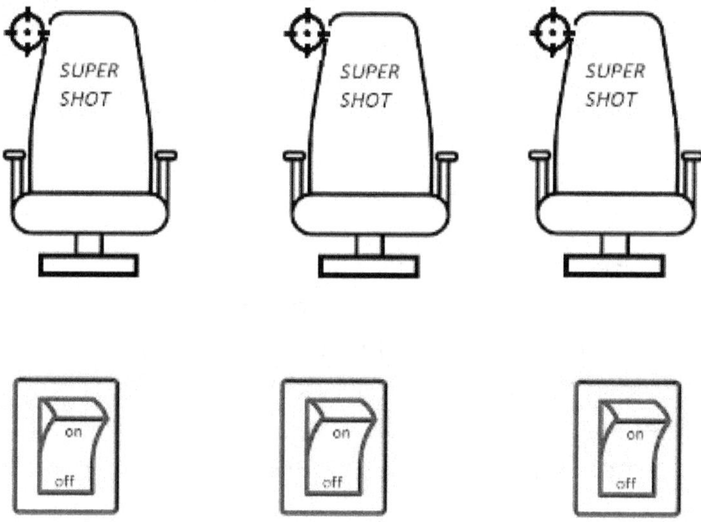

Chapter 16 - The Hexagon Maze

Check the time! Here's carriage last!
Stop the clock. When? Strike fast.
Three lives. Good timing you need to do,
Safe in the wind here's an odd clue:
Set the time, your choices are two,
Complete the hard to change the view.

Time remaining 16:08
Thinking time remaining 01:00

These are the most important sixteen minutes of my life, Tom thought to himself and a shiver ran all the way down his spine. The minute clock was already ticking down. The final puzzle, this is it. His thoughts turned briefly to Harvey and Holly trapped behind them, they would have been a help in the final carriage. Then poor

George popped in his head, until Isabelle snapped him back to the present.

"Tom, Shaun, what do we think?" said Isabelle. "Tom, hey, Tom, wake up!" Isabelle clicked her fingers awaking Tom from his thoughts.

Tom was annoyed at himself for daydreaming. He knew the final carriage would probably be the hardest.

"We have to stop a clock. Doesn't sound too difficult," said Shaun.

"Good timing… that sounds like we have to stop the clock at a particular time," said Tom.

"What does it mean 'in the wind'? Is there going to be an open window?" asked Shaun.

"I don't think so." Tom shook his head. "Why is it an odd clue? Three lives sounds to me like there could be a cage to worry about too!"

"It seems as if we have a choice. Do we fix the easy clock or the hard clock?" Isabelle pointed at the poem. "And what does it mean about the view?"

"Let's go for the easy clock and then see what we have to do," Shaun suggested.

"There's really not much help in the poem. We might as well," said Tom. "But we have only fifteen minutes so we must be quick."

"Yes, come on." Shaun jumped on the spot as the last few seconds ticked away and the door slid open.

They stepped into the final carriage and looked around.

"The exit is to the side, not at the front," observed Shaun.

"That leads out onto the platform," said Tom. "Carriage six is always different from the other five."

"We have six chairs facing the wall in that corner," gestured Isabelle.

"Clocks," observed Tom. "Lots and lots of clocks. On both walls. With a red button between each of them." Tom went over to the left where there were six digital images of clocks all moving at different speeds and some moving counter-clockwise. He turned and counted eleven clocks on the other wall.

"And in these corners, we have an identical grandfather clock and safe combo," Shaun frowned at the unusual combination of objects. "There's our safe from the poem, it's not windy though."

"The clue is in the poem. How does that help us?" asked Isabelle.

"This must be the easy option." Tom pointed to the left wall. "Six clocks against eleven on the right."

"So, we'll start on the left," suggested Shaun.

Isabelle was biting her bottom lip. "I don't get it. What do we need to do?"

Shaun started playing with the hands on the grandfather clock until Tom saw him and yelled "Stop!"

"I think if you had moved that hand too far you would have been in a cage!"

"Thanks, Tom. This Conductor guy just loves his cages." Shaun involuntarily looked up to the ceiling.

Tom walked to the chairs. "These must be for the second part of the puzzle." Each had a video games controller attached with a cable, otherwise they were ordinary. He joined Isabelle who was staring at the clocks with a worried look on her face.

"There's nothing exciting about this grandfather clock. The front doesn't open." He rapped on the glass front with his knuckle.

"There's nothing on the cabinet except for this hole." He poked his little finger into the hole. Then he peered in the hole to try and get a better look. Then he put his finger back in and twisted it.

"Look, in here there's a metal square. It feels like it will turn, but I can barely move it with my finger. There must be something to turn it with so we can set the time."

"Of course!" Isabelle yelled. "It's in the safe. It's not wind. There's no wind inside a carriage with no windows. It's wind!" She said the word to rhyme with 'kind'. "We need to wind the clock! It's 'safe in the wind'. Whatever we need to wind the clock is in the safe!"

"That's great, Issy, but how do we open this?" On the front of the safe there was a digital display and a number pad. "We need a three-digit code."

"It's something to do with these clocks, I know it is," said Isabelle, folding her arms as she stared at the clocks.

"Stop the clock!" Tom exclaimed. "From the poem. We need to stop them. That must be what the red buttons are for."

"There's a red button between each of these clocks." Tom inspected the button. "And have you noticed that these clocks are all running at different speeds?"

"There's a couple that are running backwards," said Isabelle. "This hour hand is running faster than the minute hand. That's weird."

"When do we press the button, then?" asked Shaun.

"It's in the poem, always in the poem." Tom was mumbling to himself. "Which words stand out as unusual? Strike… why is it strike? Strike a pose?"

"Is there anything odd about those clocks, other than that they are moving strangely?" Shaun looked from the clocks to Isabelle.

"At certain points, they do show the same time, but otherwise nothing I can tell."

"Yes! That's it!" Tom exclaimed so loudly he made Isabelle jump. "Strike a match, match the time! When the clocks show the same time, press the button!" He tried to watch both clocks but it was extremely difficult. "This is going to need good timing. Shaun, you watch that clock, Issy, watch this one."

"What time do you need?" asked Isabelle.

"Eight thirty. Can you count me down please?"

Isabelle's clock was running fast, Shaun's clock hour and minute hand were always the same distance apart.

"Nearly there," called Isabelle.

"Here also. Three… two… one… go!" called Shaun.

Tom pressed the button. The clock on the left stopped while the clock on the right kept going. Underneath the red button on the side of the carriage appeared the number four.

"Yes!" Isabelle jumped up and down.

"Quickly, let's get the rest done," Tom urged.

They quickly repeated the action for the remaining four buttons, giving them five numbers underneath the buttons

    4   7   3   2   1

"Five numbers and a three-digit code for the safe, but I know why!" Shaun grinned from ear to ear as he walked towards the safe and pressed three buttons. The safe popped open with a fanfare.

"There's only this metal bar," Shaun showed Tom and Isabelle. It had a wooden handle.

"How did you know that?" Tom was stunned.

Shaun laughed. "The poem says here's an 'odd' clue. I just used the odd numbers!"

"Well done," said Tom and they high fived. "But how did you know which order to put them in?"

Shaun's face fell. "I didn't even think about that. I just went from left to right."

"Well it worked," Isabelle laughed. "Now we need to set the time."

Shaun put the end of the metal bar through the hole in the grandfather clock cabinet and started turning. The minute hand of the clock started moving slowly from twelve towards one.

"Great, but what time do we set it to?" said Tom.

"I don't know. What did the poem say?" said Shaun, still turning the handle.

"It just said 'set the time'," said Isabelle. "It didn't say what time."

"If it says to set the time, let's set it as it is now," said Tom.

"Good idea, Tom, but what time is it now? We don't have our phones or watches," said Shaun.

"We can work it out," said Tom. "Issy, the Conductor doesn't like to be late so I'm sure even with George's injury we left on time. What time were we scheduled to leave, can you remember?"

"One o'clock was our departure time," said Isabelle.

"Always a great memory," Tom complimented her. "And we had fifteen minutes left when we entered the carriage.

"Right, and we had ninety minutes to start with," said Shaun. Tom and Isabelle looked at him, surprised he had remembered. He smiled and said, "It's the same length as a football match."

"Seventy-five minutes after one o'clock is two fifteen," said Isabelle.

"Great," said Shaun. He started turning the handle furiously. The clock hands moved forwards.

He stopped at two fifteen and then stood back and rubbed his hands together. Nothing happened.

"We must have been in here for five minutes, maybe its two twenty now," Isabelle said.

Tom turned the handle the other way and stopped at two twenty. The clock was bathed in green light.

In front of the six chairs the left wall of the carriage changed into a massive screen. The words 'Enter here' appeared and then the screen split into six, one view for each chair.

The three remaining puzzleteers rushed to the seats and sat down. Shaun grabbed his controller and started moving it.

"It's a maze," he called.

Tom and Isabelle grabbed their controllers and started moving.

In front of Tom was a computer-generated brick wall. He moved the controller to the left and followed the brick wall, until it ended. He went forward, turned right and walked into a dead end.

"Bah!" he called out. "This is impossible."

Shaun was also walking in to dead ends and becoming frustrated.

"I can't tell where I'm going!"

"The poem, Shaun! If we complete the hard clock then we will get a different view. Maybe it will be from the top!" Tom exclaimed. "The clue is always in the poem!"

"That will be so much easier," Shaun agreed.

"Quickly! We know what to do." They got up and rushed to the right side of the carriage. Tom and Isabelle were stopping the clocks on the wall while Shaun went to the safe.

"It's a five-digit code this time," he called. Then he found the small hole in the clock and put his little finger in.

"This is a different shape." He sounded disappointed. "We can't use the same handle."

"Argghhh!" exclaimed Isabelle as she pressed the button to stop clock six too early. A siren sounded and the Conductor's silhouette appeared on the wall.

"Two lives left! Press carefully, young Isabelle." The Conductor laughed meanly and then disappeared.

Shaun rushed to help Tom and Isabelle with the clocks. Even though they moved fast, it seemed to the three of them to take forever. Isabelle slammed the button with the palm of her hand out of frustration when the clocks eventually showed the same time again. The clock on the left stopped and the number nine appeared.

"Last one. Yes!" exclaimed Isabelle as she stopped the clocks and the tenth and last number appeared.

"Five odd numbers and five even numbers," Tom observed.

Shaun ran to the safe. "Tell me the odd numbers!"

Tom called them and Shaun tapped the numbers on the safe keypad. The safe opened up with a fanfare.

"Got it!" exclaimed Shaun and he held aloft the metal bar. Immediately he pushed it into the hole of the clock casing and started turning it furiously to get the clock to the correct time.

"It must be another three minutes from where we were," said Isabelle.

Two twenty-three, thought Tom, seven minutes to get through the maze.

The clock became bathed in green light and in front of the chairs, the image changed from the six individual views to one picture of a six-sided maze from the top down. Above the maze was a timer showing 06:52 remaining.

"A hexagon maze." Tom stared at the image until Shaun shook him into action.

"Come, let's go!" He slapped Tom's shoulder as he ran to the chair and grabbed the controller.

At each of the six corners of the maze was a picture of one of the puzzleteers. Even George was there, smiling.

"That's going to make it so much easier." Tom sat down between Shaun and Isabelle and grabbed his controller. He looked at the maze, which filled the wall from top to bottom and was the same size from left to right, and tried to trace a path to the middle. He gave up and started moving his image from the top corner.

Shaun started moving his picture. "I guess we have to get to the square in the middle?" he said.

"That's where I'm going." Tom moved his image into the maze.

"Why is the inside half colored orange and the outside half gray?" Isabelle asked as she too moved her character.

Time remaining 05:21.

The three were quiet, concentrating on getting through the maze. Occasionally there was a groan or sigh of frustration as they found yet another dead-end.

Shaun was making the best progress through the maze. Tom came to a dead end and he had to move a long way back to find a new path. Isabelle was making slow but steady progress.

They felt the train beginning to slow. Tom had been so engrossed in the puzzles he had hardly thought about the fact he was travelling in a train.

Time remaining 04:03.

"The train's slowing down, Issy. We're near the end." He knew their time was running out. The thought spurred him on. He had to get to the middle.

Shaun was the first to move into the orange section of the maze. There was a siren and a red light flashed.

"No, you can't cage me for that, I didn't do anything!" Shaun shouted.

"Hahaha!" The Conductor's laugh was loud and slow and thumped through Tom's chest. His voice filled the carriage. "No cage, young Shaun, not unless you get caught by the mini-conductors. One for each of you! Oh, and by the way, you only have three minutes left before we reach our destination!" He laughed again, unpleasantly.

In the corners where Tom, Isabelle and Shaun's pictures had been, there appeared a picture of the Conductor from the shoulders up. As usual, a yellow light was behind him, casting his face and brimmed hat into a black silhouette.

The mini-conductor from where Shaun started entered the maze. It moved quickly, but also randomly, heading down dead ends and turning around but progressively getting closer to the centre.

"We need to hurry!" shouted Tom, as he moved into the orange section accompanied by a siren, which made the mini-Conductor start to move from where his picture had been.

"Yes!" Isabelle exclaimed through gritted teeth and accompanied by a third siren just seconds after signified that Isabelle also entered the orange section. Her mini-conductor came to life and started to give chase.

"You stay away from me," she yelled at her mini-conductor as she moved her character closer to the middle of the maze.

"You're nearly there, Issy," Tom glanced at Isabelle's character before steering his around a series of turns.

"There's only one entrance to the middle," she called out as she moved her character to the entrance at the bottom.

"Yes!" she jumped up and yelled, making both Tom and Shaun jump.

'SAFE' appeared on the screen in green letters and the mini-conductor chasing her froze on the screen.

'PHEW!' She heaved a massive sigh of relief. "I've completed carriage six!" She started jumping around the carriage in joy.

Time remaining 02:01.

She stopped jumping and turned to watch the screen where Shaun and Tom were frantically manoeuvring their pictures towards the centre of the maze.

"Come on, you can do it!" she cheered them on.

Tom's character was nearly in the middle. One more turn would take him to the top of the square.

"Where did he come from!" Tom nearly screamed as the mini-conductor appeared blocking his route to the center. Tom had to move his picture back up and around, the mini-conductor hot on his heels.

"Yours is stuck," Isabelle jumped on the spot as the mini-conductor chasing Shaun was trying to get out of a dead-end. "The middle is right there. You're going to do it!"

Time remaining 01:15.

Shaun ignored her and turned his character away from the square.

"What are you doing?" called Isabelle.

Tom was desperately trying to escape his mini-conductor, who was hot on heels and determined to catch him. They moved at the same speed and Tom knew any mistakes and he would be caught.

He went up and away from the middle. He turned diagonally left, then right, then right again so he was heading back to the middle.

"Lost him!"He clenched his fist. But the mini-conductor was taking a different route.

"Tom! He's going to intercept you," Isabelle cried.

"No, I can make it," Tom's character was coming down, whilst the mini-conductor was closing from the left. Tom was banking on getting past the junction first.

"You're not going to make it," yelled Shaun.

Tom was sweating, his heart was beating hard. "I just need to make it past this junction," he said through gritted teeth.

"I'm coming, Tom," called Shaun, and he moved his character up the same path Tom was moving down. The mini-conductor's path would merge with their path. The three of them were heading to the junction together.

Isabelle was watching, mouth open.

Shaun's character reached the junction just ahead of Tom's. He turned left and ran his character straight into the mini-conductor.

Immediately the lights went out, the siren sounded and the red flashing light went on in the top corner of the carriage. A cage dropped down and trapped Shaun where he was sitting. The lights came back on. On the carriage wall to the left of the maze, the number ten appeared in large numbers and started counting down. Tom's character passed the junction barely half a second later.

The Conductor's image appeared on the wall. Unusually, he wasn't laughing. Instead a hint of admiration was in his deep booming voice.

"A noble sacrifice, young Shaun, ten minutes in the cage for you, though!"

"N-o-o-o! Shaun, what have you done?" called Isabelle, her head in her hands.

Tom turned to look at Shaun in the cage, mouth open. He stopped moving his character.

"Don't stop!" Shaun yelled from his cage. "Get to the middle! There can't be much time left!"

Tom turned and looked at the maze, moved his character down, then right, around the middle square and through the entrance at the bottom. The word 'SAFE' appeared.

Tom had done it!

The maze on the screen disappeared, replaced with the words, 'Congratulations, Tom and Isabelle!' The timer showed just forty-three seconds left.

"Shaun, what did you do?" Tom turned to face Shaun in the cage, still sitting on the chair. "I can't believe you did that, thank you so much!"

"Yes, Shaun. That was amazing!" added Isabelle.

"Tom, mate, even when I was grumpy when we first met, you were fair to me. You helped me in the beginning and explained what was going on. You didn't judge me because I didn't want to be here. You were a good buddy."

Tom was taken aback. He didn't realise he had made such an impact on Shaun.

"You're welcome. I was just trying to help."

"You did help. Thank you, Tom."

"But you didn't have to sacrifice yourself like that. Now you won't be able to go through to the station puzzle."

"I think I've had enough puzzles for one day," Shaun laughed. "Tom, that's why you deserve to go through. You love this show. I hadn't even watched it."

"What about the prize?" asked Tom.

"Is there a prize?" Shaun looked through the bars of the cage. "I had no idea. But you had better win it, now."

"I'll share it with you, Shaun," Tom's face was full of determination.

"Thanks, Tom. My team could really do with some new facilities."

They could feel the train coming to a stop. Shaun reached his hand through the bars of the cage. Tom took it and shook it.

"Good luck, Tom, good luck, Isabelle. Wait, where's the key?"

The clock counted to zero, the train stopped and the door in the right corner opened on its own.

"I guess we don't need a key this time," said Tom.

Tom and Isabelle started walking towards the door.

"This was better than football," Shaun called from his cage. He gave them a thumbs-up through the bars.

Isabelle waved to Shaun and walked through the door.

"See you soon."

Tom followed but looked back to Shaun in the cage.

"Thanks, mate. That's one of the nicest things I think anyone has ever done for me."

He stepped through the door towards the final station puzzle.

Help Tom, Isabelle and Shaun through the Hexagon maze.

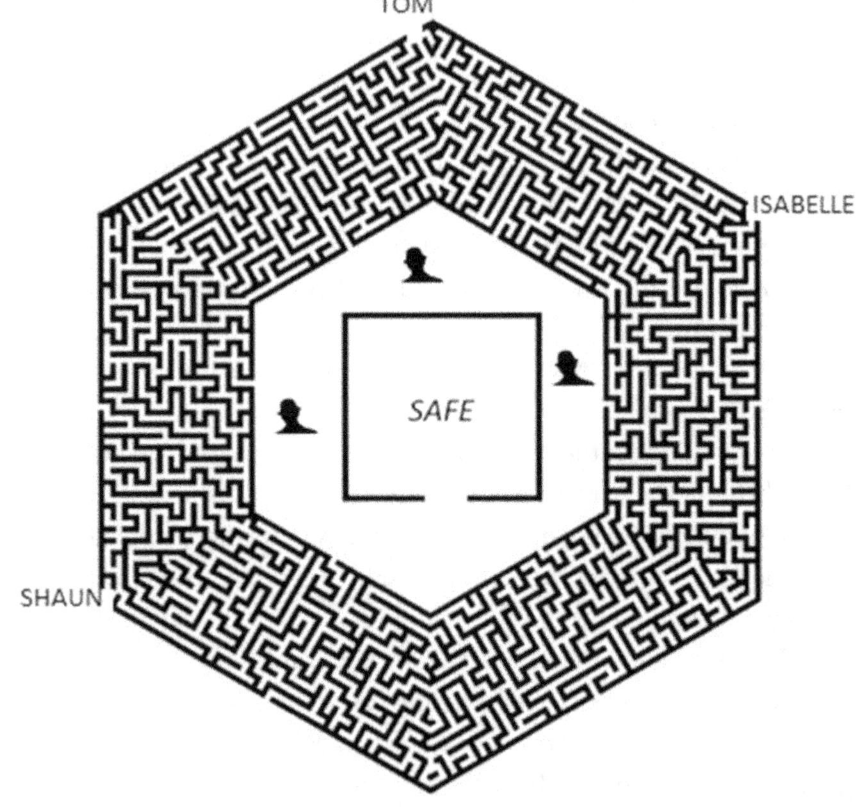

Chapter 17 – A Final Interview

The door closed automatically behind Tom and Isabelle once they left the carriage as Shaun looked on from his cage. There was nothing else he could do.

He looked around the carriage. His timer was still ticking down and showed over eight minutes still to go. The hexagon maze and clocks around the walls disappeared, leaving plain white walls with red buttons.

Shaun smiled to himself. He was happy he had helped Tom achieve his dream. Team work. His coach would be proud. After a few moments, the cage lifted and the maze image disappeared. Shaun stretched his arms and his legs, relieved to be let out of the cage early. He heard a friendly female voice which he recognised as Jenny's.

"Thank you for participating in the Puzzle Train. Congratulations on getting all the way to carriage six."

"Cool, what happens next?" Shaun said to the ceiling.

"Please make your way back through the carriages to the rear of the train. The doors are all open for you," explained Jenny and at that moment the door back to carriage five slid open.

Shaun headed back through the door, through carriage five, past the Super Shots. There was no sign of Holly and Harvey.

Through carriage four, past the exercise bikes and the chess pieces. In carriage three, Shaun looked at the maze of pipes without stopping. He went on into carriage two and the different colored tiles and, finally, into carriage one with its wall full of little boxes.

Shaun made sure he got a good look at each carriage as he walked through. He wanted to remember his time on the Puzzle Train.

He stopped by the boxes around the spot where he first got trapped in the cage and thought how impatient he had been, and he laughed to himself. He stepped out of the back of carriage one and onto the balcony and he thought of George getting his ankle trapped and not being able to take part. The steps that he had come up an hour and a half ago had been moved to the side so he could walk down them onto the platform.

The station they had arrived at was much smaller than the one they left. The train stretched along the full length of the platform and there was no roof. Shaun could see the blue sky and feel the warmth of the sun and a slight breeze on his face. There were no signs that gave a clue as to where they were.

Jenny was on the platform waiting to greet him with her familiar clipboard, her headphones and microphone. She was talking into her microphone. "Yes, he's here… yup, I'll bring him… no problem."

She turned to Shaun.

"Hi, Shaun, well done! Carriage six is a fantastic achievement!" She shook his hand. "Now please come with me. It's time for our final interviews in the waiting room." She walked off quickly down the platform towards the front of the train.

Shaun followed Jenny. He looked at the carriages as he walked past. They seemed so plain in beige with purple numbers, totally disguising the puzzles within. The front of the train was blocked from view by a blue screen that ran the width of the platform.

Jenny held open the waiting room door and Shaun entered the small building and rushed over to Holly and Harvey in their green jumpsuits amongst a group of people who he assumed were technical and production crew.

"What happened to you? We were hoping you would join us in the final carriage." Shaun joined Holly and Harvey.

"After we were let out of the cages, all our scores were reset. Poor Hols couldn't get the hang of the Super Shot and I tried to help her as much as possible but we just couldn't shoot that final plane and get the key," Harvey explained.

Holly looked at Harvey, "Thanks for helping, Harvey. I really appreciate it." She turned to Shaun. "Where are Tom and Isabelle?"

"They made it through! They went through the door at the side!" said Shaun.

"Oh wow! They're going to do the station puzzle!" said Holly, jumping up and down and clapping.

"What was the final puzzle?" asked Harvey.

Shaun explained the final puzzle, although he didn't tell them he sacrificed himself for Tom in the digital maze.

"OK, everyone, come here please, towards me. You three, line up. Yes, that's it." Jenny was waving her arms, directing people with her clipboard, trying to organise the final shots for the show. "Okay, ready for Marvin."

"There we are, our three amazing puzzleteers!" Right on cue, Marvin made a grand entrance and held his arms out in greeting. "Carriage six! What an achievement!"

Marvin shook each of them by the hand. "Well, team, that was breath-taking. Fantastic, well done!" He then turned to look at the camera.

"First things first. We have good news about George. We have heard from the hospital. X-ray results are in and his ankle is not broken, just badly sprained, so a few days' rest and he will be jumping up and down and falling over like before!" He paused for breath and looked at the relieved faces of Holly, Harvey and Shaun before continuing.

"Shaun," Marvin put his hands on his heart, "that was amazing. But first, Holly, Harvey," he tilted his head towards them, "you guys really struggled in carriage five. Holly, what went wrong?"

"Those super shots were really hard to control. I was grateful to Harvey for helping me out."

"And Harvey, what was your high point today?"

"I enjoyed all of it, but my favorite was definitely the maze of pipes. I really enjoyed that puzzle."

"Yes," agreed Marvin. "You certainly took control there." He turned to Shaun.

"Shaun, that was one of the biggest sacrifices I can remember in five hundred episodes. What made you do it?" Marvin's eyed were wide and glistening. Harvey and Holly looked at him confused.

"Tom was really kind to me all day. He loves the Puzzle Train way more than I do and he will appreciate going on far more than I ever would."

"Wow, what did you do, Shaun?" said Holly.

"I'll tell you later," Shaun smiled.

"Now, we have our souvenir carriages for you. Holly and Harvey with a number five on them. Not many people get these. And Shaun, your souvenir has a six on and even fewer people get these!" He winked at the camera as one of the production staff passed him the trains so he could award them, with a shake of the hand, to Holly, Harvey and Shaun.

Marvin turned to the camera. "Well, there we are. Three fantastic puzzleteers who came so close to beating our Conductor. Now, let's go and see how Tom and Isabelle get on with the final station puzzle."

"Would you like to watch?" asked Jenny as she gestured to a TV attached to the wall. All three of them excitedly said yes and gathered around the screen to watch their two new friends in the final puzzle.

Chapter 18 – The Station Puzzle

Tom and Isabelle stepped off the train onto a concrete floor. They were in a narrow corridor. A brick wall was to their left, a blue canvas screen on their right. Ahead was a green door.

"This is the platform," said Tom. "Issy, do you realise we're about to go to the station puzzle! Hardly anyone gets this far!" He was shaking with excitement. They walked towards the door. As they approached a poem and two clocks appeared.

> Congratulations on completing the train.
> One more puzzle awaits. What a pain!
> Remember the train and follow the clues,
> Don't be hasty, your freedom you'll lose.
> Lots of things... don't be fazed.
> Where were you before the maze?
>
> Time remaining 10:00
> Thinking time remaining 01:00

The minute clock started ticking down. The clock showing ten minutes didn't.

"Ten minutes starts once we go inside," Tom muttered to Isabelle. "The maze was carriage six. Before that we were in carriage five."

"Yes, the Super Shots," agreed Isabelle.

"There's not much else in the poem that helps," said Tom.

"We have to follow the clues. I hope that makes sense once we get in there."

"I guess we will find out soon. Good luck, Issy!"

"Good luck, Tom!"

The minute clock clicked to zero, the door automatically opened inwards and Tom and Isabelle walked inside, full of nervous anticipation. They were both stunned by what they saw.

"What a mess!" Tom felt deflated as he surveyed the large room in front of him. Behind him, the door automatically slammed shut, kicking up dust as it dragged across the carpet.

"And the smell." Isabelle screwed her nose up. "It's like no one has been in here for years."

There were no windows. The walls were covered in framed paintings, pictures, several calendars and clocks. The walls were painted beige, which was now faded and grimy in places.

They walked across the room on the thin green carpet, avoiding piles of debris and old bits of furniture.

"This is the way to the Conductor's office." Tom tried the handle of the only other door which didn't turn.

"Here's a card reader." Isabelle looked at the small metal object under the handle. "No key needed."

"We need to get a move on. Where do we start?" Tom looked back at the room.

In the middle of the room there was a large wooden desk piled high with newspapers and magazines, a desk lamp, an old-fashioned fan and a telephone.

"No-one has tidied this place in years. What can you remember about the other station puzzles?" asked Isabelle, as she looked at a large white sink on top of a cupboard. Above the sink was a complicated series of water pipes. Next to that was a small fridge with a metal kettle and tea, coffee and sugar jars on top of it.

"I can't remember." Tom's mind went blank. He had watched all the station puzzles many times but now under the pressure, his memory was letting him down.

To their right were six filing cabinets against the wall in a row, beige with metal handles. Tall wooden shelves stood against the wall full of files with faded labels, some turning yellow with age.

Cluttering up much of the rest of the floor were waste paper baskets, office chairs, a series of gardening tools, and an empty hat standing next to a variety of plastic potted plants. There was a large green floor safe, with a smaller safe on top of it.

"The only clue is what we did before the maze, but there's nothing in here that looks like a Super Shot." Isabelle stared around the cluttered room.

"There's not even any wires to connect, like we had to do in carriage five," Tom said. "Wait, Issy. Before the maze, we were setting clocks!"

"Clocks! Yes, Tom, that's it. There's one on the wall here," called Isabelle.

"There's a small one on the desk," said Tom. "One on the filing cabinets."

"A watch on the sink. I don't think we'll need that." Isabelle pulled the clock off the wall. It was the size of a dinner plate and took both her hands to retrieve it from its fixing.

"I can't see any more," said Tom.

"Look at the time. It says it's two twenty-four. That must be a good sign, Tom. That's the same time we had to set the clock in carriage six."

Isabelle turned the clock over. It had a solid back except for a small hole. Tom put his finger in the hole and pulled the back of the clock off. Inside there was a piece of paper folded up into four. Tom grabbed it and unfolded it.

> Well done you found me,
> Now what did you do in carriage three?

"Carriage three was the pipes, Issy." Tom flicked the piece of paper with his fingers.

"Right! we had to direct the balls down to lift the key. You got trapped in the cage."

"Oh, yes." Tom went red.

"Pipes. I've seen some pipes, Tom. Over there." Isabelle pointed to the sink and they rushed over.

Above the sink, reaching to the ceiling, was a complicated pattern of pipes with many different junctions and levers.

"What do we need to do, do you think?" asked Tom.

Isabelle pointed to a valve right at the top. "Too high to reach."

"It's set to the off position." Tom craned his neck to get a better view.

He looked down. "Hey, Issy, this is weird. Taps normally have an 'H' and a 'C' for hot and cold on them but these have a 'W' and an 'R' on them. What does that mean?"

"I'm not sure, Tom, but I think we use these levers to divert the water down to the taps. I don't know which one. Maybe even to both?"

Tom investigated the sink further. There was a plughole but no plug. Underneath was a white wooden cupboard with a silver handle. Tom bent down and pulled on the handle but it wouldn't open. He stood up and looked at the taps again.

"The one with the 'R' on is on the right, but 'W' isn't left." Isabelle turned both taps but nothing happened.

"That's it, Issy! 'R' for right, 'W' is for wrong! We must make the water come out of the 'R' tap."

"Yes, of course. Well done, Tom. You get a chair to stand on so you can reach that valve. I'll work out the route the water will take."

Tom rushed over to the desk and grabbed the chair that was behind it. It was on wheels so he was able to push it easily over to the sink.

Isabelle was tracing a path with her finger. At some of the junctions she would change the tap so the water would flow the other way. Some of the taps were already facing the right way.

"OK, Tom, I'm happy. You go up there and change the valve. I'll hold the chair."

Tom climbed on top of the chair and wobbled a little bit but was able to stand up on his toes reached the valve. He twisted it to the 'on' position.

"I can hear the water through the pipes.," He looked down to Isabelle. No water came out of the 'R' tap though. "Why didn't it work?"

"Wait, I need to turn the tap on." She twisted the tap and water came gushing through, into the sink and straight down the plughole.

"What now?" Tom clambered down off the chair. Before Isabelle could reply there was a 'click'. The cupboard door underneath the sink opened and the water stopped automatically. Tom bent down quickly to investigate.

"There's loads of junk in here!"

"Quick, get it out and put it here on the desk. There must be a clue somewhere."

Isabelle pushed some of the newspapers aside on the desk to make room. Tom passed the items from the cupboard to Isabelle and she laid them neatly on the desk. There was a bottle of bleach, a packet of cards, a toilet roll, a yellow ball, a rock, two DVD cases, a shoe and a candle.

They opened the packet of playing cards. There was no clue there, and the DVD cases were empty. Tom bounced the ball on the desk in frustration.

"Where's the clue, Issy?"

Unexpectedly a voice boomed through the room. It was the Conductor.

"You have six minutes left!"

"Six minutes! Is that all?"

"Wait, Tom. In carriage three we used balls to get the key. This ball sounded hollow!"

"Yes look, there's a line here." Tom twisted the ball and it split in half. Inside was the clue.

> Afourmentioned care,
> Black and white square.

"What does that mean?" asked Tom.

Isabelle stared at the clue and shook her head.

They looked at each other and then stared from the piece of paper around the room. Is this as far as we go? Tom thought to himself.

"Is it a reference back to the train?" Tom frowned. "What is aforementioned anyway?"

"Something that has been mentioned before. Wait, it's spelt wrong. It should be F O R E not F O U R."

"Carriage four, that was full of black and white squares," Tom exclaimed.

"Yes," exclaimed Isabelle. "Find a chessboard."

She was already searching the desk, Tom went to the top of the filing cabinets.

"Yes!" Tom yelled. "Here it is, Issy. Look on the back."

> Water, water all around, not a drop to drink;
> That's the clue, what do you think?

"Is it the sink again?" asked Tom.

"I don't think so. You can drink the water from the tap." Isabelle thought for a second, frowning. "It's part of an old poem referring to the sea. Look for something to do with the ocean."

Tom looked at the furniture, filing cabinet, desk and shelves. There was nothing obvious there. Isabelle was looking at the walls.

"Look here, Tom. Here's a map of the world. That has all the oceans on it."

"Could be… wait, look here, Issy. Here's a picture of a sailing ship on the ocean." Tom pulled the picture off the hook on the wall.

"Yes, that's even better." She joined Tom looking at the picture. They turned the picture around to look at the back of it.

"Here it is, Tom. The clue is taped onto the back of the picture. Hold still." Isabelle pulled the clue off and read it out to Tom.

> That's four puzzles down and don't you doubt it.
> Find today's date and read all about it.

"'Read all about it!' Isn't that what newspaper sellers used to shout in the olden days?" said Tom.

"Yes!" Isabelle was already running to the desk. "Here's a pile of newspapers. Find the one with today's date."

Isabelle grabbed half of the newspapers off the desk and handed them to Tom.

"That's loads. There must be thirty here," complained Tom.

"Well stop moaning and get on with it. I'll go through this pile. The dates are at the top here." Isabelle held up the nearest newspaper and pointed to the date. There were about thirty newspapers each.

"What is today's date?" asked Tom.

"Saturday twenty-second of May." Isabelle rolled her eyes.

They started searching through the pile of newspapers. There were many different ones, but all had the date on the front, some recent, some old and some of the dates were even in the future. Tom picked up one dated twenty years in the future. The headline read 'Popular TV show the Puzzle Train now using flying trains.' Tom chuckled.

"Tom, no time for that. Keep checking!" Isabelle snapped whilst searching through her pile of newspapers. "No!" She stamped her foot. "I don't have today's date here."

Tom finished his pile of newspapers. "I don't have today's date either, Issy," he said, clearly disappointed.

"What do we do, Tom? There can only be about four minutes left!"

"Wait! There's a calendar on the wall over there." Tom ran towards it.

The calendar was open at December and had a picture of a steam train going through a snow-covered field with some old houses in the distance. Tom pulled it off the wall and started looking through it.

"It's not this, Issy. This is from three years ago!"

Tom threw the calendar down on the floor in frustration and then thought about the headline he had read in the future newspaper.

"Wait, it's a trick! We don't need today's date. We need the date when everyone is watching us."

Isabelle stared at him, hands on hips. "What?"

"We're filming today but the show won't be on TV until next Tuesday! No. Wait! The Tuesday after that! That's the date we need. What's that date?"

"First of June," replied Isabelle. "Quick, let's go and check for that date!"

Tom and Isabelle frantically searched through the pile of newspapers again.

"Here it is!" Isabelle held the paper up triumphantly, then laid it out on the desk. The front-page headline was something about a new species of fish being found in the deepest part of the ocean.

"That's not it." She turned the page and found what they were looking for across pages two and three, in large black print.

> Remember back to carriage one;
> Since then we've had sum fun.
> The final entry! Think hard,
> That will reveal the location of the key card!

Carriage one seems like a lifetime ago, thought Tom. He remembered his first tentative steps onto the train and all the boxes and keys.

"That was the one with all the boxes," Tom said.

"I wonder why they've spelt 'some' wrong? Look it's spelt S U M, not S O M E."

"That must be a clue. The Conductor wouldn't make a mistake like that by accident." He stared into space for a few seconds gathering his thoughts. "Hmm… carriage one… yes, the first box was a spade. I remember I was so nervous to open that box."

"Right, what else was there? A football pitch, a book, a picture of a man." Isabelle counted the clues off on her fingers.

"That wasn't a man, in the end. And a baker."

"Then we put the code numbers onto that screen."

"Yes, one four four was the last code."

Their thinking was interrupted by the Conductor's voice booming through the room.

"There are only three minutes Puzzling Time left!"

"Three minutes, Issy! One puzzle. We can do this!"

"We need to move fast." Isabelle was beginning to panic.

"One hundred and forty-four." Tom was looking round muttering one four four under his breath. There was nothing on any of the paintings or on the filing cabinets or the desk. He opened the desk drawer, it was empty.

Isabelle was rushing around the room desperately looking at everything. Then she saw the rake and then the spade.

"Look, Tom, a spade! That was the final clue. A spade! It was a spade on a playing card but here's a real spade!"

"Issy, just wait…" Tom started to say, but it was already too late.

Isabelle picked up the spade, but it was one of the Conductor's tricks. The lights went out, the siren sounded, the red light flashed in the corner of the room and from nowhere a cage dropped over Isabelle. On one of the walls appeared the Conductor's silhouette and the number five.

The Conductor's deep voice filled the room.

"So close and yet so far, Isabelle. You did so well! Such a shame to be trapped at the last hurdle."

"N-o-o-o-o-o-o!" screamed Tom, close to tears. "Let her out! Let her out! We're so close!" He grabbed the cage and started shaking it as hard as he could. It wouldn't move an inch.

"Young Tom, you know that's not the way the game works," snapped the Conductor. "By the way you have less than two minutes now."

"It's not fair!" yelled Tom.

The Conductor's silhouette disappeared.

"Tom! Focus!" shouted Isabelle from the cage and stamped her foot in frustration. She had a lump in her throat and tears in her eyes.

"Issy, you won't meet the Conductor! Even if I complete the puzzle there're only two minutes left and you'll be in there for five."

"Yes, I know. It's my own stupid fault I got caught in here." Isabelle's voice was full of frustration and her head was down. "But you can still go and meet the Conductor. But only if you focus!" she yelled at him. She felt a little better for taking her frustrations out on Tom.

Her tone spurred Tom into action.

"Right, Issy. The real spade was a trick. So maybe it is the spades from playing cards."

"Good, Tom."

"We found a pack of cards when we emptied out the cupboard beneath the sink," Tom remembered, excitement rushing through him. He hurried over to the desk where they had emptied the items from the cupboard. The desk was covered in newspapers, but Tom quickly threw them on the floor and found the pack of cards. He opened it up and emptied all the cards on the desk, frantically sorting out all the spades.

"Hey, Issy, the poem says a key card. I bet that means that one of these cards is the key."

"You're right, Tom," said Isabelle from her cage. "That's why it's a card reader to go through the door and not a metal key."

"But which one, Issy? One or four? There isn't a 'one' card, just an ace. Do you think that's it, the ace? Or is it the four because four appears twice?"

"One minute to go!" boomed the Conductor.

"Breathe, Tom, and relax. A minute to go, all you need to do is find the right card and put it in the reader," Isabelle said calmly from the cage.

Tom took a deep breath. His gran would be so proud they had got this far. The clue is always in the poem he thought to himself. He read the poem again.

"Sum, Issy! That's the answer! S U M! We have to add them up. One and four and four is nine. It's the nine of spades that opens the door! I know it!"

"Do it, Tom, quickly! See if it opens the door!"

Tom sorted through the cards and found the nine of spades. The card was the identical weight, size and shape as all the others. There was no way of knowing whether it was the right card.

"If I'm wrong, Issy, there's a cage waiting for me."

"Thirty seconds," called the Conductor.

"There's no time, Tom! You may as well go for it!" Isabelle called, bouncing up and down with excitement, as much as she could in her cage.

Tom walked over to the door and placed the nine of spades face down into the slot on the card reader.

The lights went out.

A siren sounded.

But it was not a red light that flashed from the corner of the room. It was a green light!

The door clicked and swung open. Tom breathed a sigh of relief, then jumped up, punching the air and shouted "Y-e-e-e-e-e-s!"

"Well done, Tom!" Isabelle clapped from her cage.

"Congratulations, young Tom!" boomed the Conductor. "Come through to my office!"

Tom went over to Isabelle in her cage.

"Issy, I can't believe it. I had hoped so much we would go and meet the Conductor together. You are so amazing. We wouldn't have got halfway through without you."

"It's my own stupid fault." She sounded annoyed, frustrated and sad, but she put on a brave face for Tom. "Now go and see the Conductor! If anyone deserves to complete the Puzzle Train, it's you. All those hours you spent watching and re-watching."

"Time to go, Tom." The Conductor's voice boomed impatiently through the room. Tom walked away from the cage and started towards the door.

"Tell me all about it later!" Isabelle called as Tom stepped through the door.

"Will do. See you later. Thanks for all your help, Issy." Tom called back as he walked through the door which closed automatically behind him.

Chapter 19 -The Conductor

Tom stepped into a small well-lit corridor. At the end of it was a green wooden door, plain except for a brass handle and a brass sign with black writing which read:

'The Conductor – knock three times and enter.'

Tom couldn't believe it. He would be the first person ever to enter the Conductor's office in five hundred episodes of the Puzzle Train. He had spent much of the day feeling nervous and excited, but that was nothing compared to this moment.

He could feel his heart thumping in his chest, his stomach was in knots, and he had a lump in his throat that felt as if he had swallowed a tennis ball. He was breathing very quickly and his hands were sweaty.

'OK, Tom, get a grip and calm down. This is the biggest moment of your life. Enjoy it. Don't worry. First thing is to take a deep breath, hold it and count to ten.' The voice in Tom's head was not his own but that of his gran. It was so clear it was almost as if she was standing there beside him.

He took a deep breath, held it, counted to ten and then let it out. He rapped his knuckles on the door.

Knock… knock… knock.

The instruction was to enter so he turned the handle and pushed the door open. He slowly stepped through.

What greeted Tom on the other side of the door was the exact scene he had seen thousands of times on TV and the internet and he recognised it immediately. It was the Conductor's office.

The large desk was directly in front of him with a bright yellow light coming from behind it. The items on the desk, so familiar to Tom from his constant hours of studying, watching and trying to analyse who the Conductor was, cast shadows on the wall. Behind the desk a high-backed chair was facing away from Tom. Poking over from the top of the chair, Tom could see the brim of the Conductor's hat. His heart skipped a beat. There was a small chair in front of the desk as well. Tom wasn't sure whether to sit on it or not.

Tom paused. Held his breath. What next? Then a deep booming voice spoke, thumping in Tom's chest. A shiver ran all the way down Tom's spine.

"Sit!"

Tom did as he was told.

The chair turned slowly as the Conductor came face-to-face with Tom. Frustratingly for Tom, there was still no way to tell what he looked like.

"Congratulations, Tom! After eleven years and five hundred episodes, you are the very first winner of the Puzzle Train. My search is over."

Tom swallowed hard. "Th-th-thank you, Mr. C-C-Conductor," he stammered nervously. "The search for what?"

"Three thousand puzzleteers have put themselves up against *my* puzzles and every one of them has failed. My search was to find a winner. Someone with logic, determination and patience. Someone who deserved the rewards that I can offer them."

There was a pause.

"Ask of me whatever you wish to have for your prize, up to the value of five million dollars."

Tom cleared his throat.

"You know the rules of the game, young Tom. You may ask anything of me. But it can't be money and you have to be specific."

Tom knew what he wanted to ask. There was one question that had been burning away at him ever since he had watched the first episode of the Puzzle Train, but he wasn't sure if he was allowed to do so, so instead he said, "Well, I do have a list."

"Ask away. If it is within my power to give it to you, then I will."

"What I really want is for my gran to come and live near us again. There's a great house for sale near to Isabelle's. It's way bigger than our house. There would be room for all of us," Tom blurted out excitedly.

"I will buy you your house, Tom."

"Can we have new furniture?" he asked. "Oh, and the latest games consoles and games? Please buy Mom a new car. Hers is so embarrassing! It even broke down this morning."

"Yes, Tom, one of my staff will go with you to the stores and car dealership and buy whatever you would like."

"There's a field near us. Please can you buy that for Isabelle so she can have a pony? Oh, and a pony? And food for the pony and horse stuff."

"Yes. I will speak to the owner and see if it's for sale."

"Oh, and something for Shaun. He really helped me. Maybe new football stuff for his team. What do footballers need? Footballs and kit and that kind of stuff. And he said they needed their changing rooms fixed up." Tom, focus, his grans voice was in his head again.

"Oh, and can you get rid of Phil? The house would be so much nicer if you could!"

"No, Tom, that I can't do. That is not within my power."

"Oh, that's a shame," Tom said sadly.

"Is there anything else, Tom?"

Tom blurted it out without thinking but he couldn't help it. He could keep it bottled in no longer. He was desperate to know.

"Who are you, what do you look like and what do you do all day?"

"My real name has been kept secret for many years and will continue to be so." The Conductor sounded angry. Then his voice became softer before tailing away. "There are too many who would love to know…"

There was a pause and Tom instantly thought he had made a mistake. However, after a few seconds, the Conductor spoke again:

"Tom, you have impressed me throughout your journey on the train. I was beginning to wonder if I had selected the wrong child when you were so quiet at the beginning."

Tom felt his cheeks redden.

"I was pleased when you finally found your voice. I will grant you what you wish."

Tom was taken aback by the kind words the Conductor had said to him. Why couldn't Phil be like that sometimes?

The Conductor leant over and reached into his desk drawer and pulled out a small remote control. He pressed a series of buttons and the lights behind him began to fade and the main lights in the office began to get brighter. Tom realised he was finally going to see who the Conductor really was.

When the lights finally came up, the Conductor removed his wide-brimmed hat and placed it on the desk. He was not what Tom had expected. His head was shaved and his face was thin and pale and had a sharpness to it that Tom found frightening. His large eyebrows seemed to be in a permanent frown and underneath his eyes were so dark brown they were almost black. Tom could almost feel them piercing right through him as they stared at him intensely. The left eye was smaller than the right, because of a large scar that ran the length of his face from his eye to the left side of his chin. He looked old and menacing, but wise at the same time. His forehead and eyes were wrinkled, his chin was unshaven and he had the kind of mouth that looked as if it didn't smile much.

He was dressed in a white shirt and a blue jacket. His hands looked old too, his fingers were long and thin and the skin rough. Probably from years of creating puzzles, Tom thought.

"I've seen the rumors Tom. I'm not a rocket scientist, former President or sports star. I've never been a brain surgeon or an astronaut. Or, as someone suggested on their application, an alien."

Tom squirmed in his seat at the memory of his application.

"I just follow my dream. I build puzzles." The Conductor's voice was still deep but nowhere near as deep as it was on the show.

"Do you use voice effects on the show?" said Tom.

"Of course. Total disguise. Silhouette and fake voice."

Tom looked at the Conductor. "Wait a minute. I've met you before, but when?"

"I was your driver this morning, Tom."

"But you didn't have a scar then."

"I have developed many technologies over the years, including one to change my appearance for a short time." He paused and then added quietly, almost to himself, "I fear that others may have stolen it."

"Why did you drive me? How did you know where we'd be?"

"I … I had a hunch you wouldn't be at home. And I wanted to meet you. I sometimes do it with the adults as well, especially if I think someone is special enough to challenge my puzzles. I like to drive them and chat to them."

The Conductor paused, frowned, and then added, "Let's keep that as our little secret though." It was not a request.

"Of course," said Tom. "Did you really think I was special?" Tom was surprised.

"Yes, I did Tom. And hearing the way you spoke about your stepfather," he paused, "it put me in mind of… hmm…" His voice tailed off before he finished his sentence.

Tom looked at him, confused.

"I am also told you visit the website almost more than anyone else."

Tom went red. Perhaps Isabelle was right and he did go on there too often.

"It reminds me of the way things were for me when I was your age, Tom. Nothing I did was ever good enough!"

"But you're amazing, the things you create. You have the biggest quiz show on TV!" Tom was genuinely astounded.

"Thank you, Tom," said the Conductor quietly.

"But didn't you know about Darren? It was supposed to be his little brother Shaun. We've been calling him Shaun all day!"

The Conductor laughed, not the booming laugh that Tom was used to, but a dry, humorless laugh.

"Yes, I knew. The researcher phoned me from their house last night and I spoke to Shaun, Darren and their parents. Shaun was too young but I liked his brother, Darren, and their dad was very apologetic. I decided to let Darren on instead."

"Did you have to trap me in the cage?" Tom said with a smile.

"Yes, Tom, you had to learn patience and you had to learn that sometimes things aren't always as easy as they seem. And you did learn, otherwise you wouldn't be standing here now," the Conductor answered impatiently.

"Did you have to trap Isabelle in the cage? She was so close to coming through to meet you too. I would never have got as far without her."

"Yes, Tom. The spade was always going to trigger a cage. I can't change the rules just because it's the final puzzle."

"Where are the others now? Where's Isabelle?"

"They're with Marvin. Isabelle has been released and is having her final interview."

"Can I see what she's saying?"

"No. Enough, now Tom!" the Conductor shouted. "Enough questions!" Tom was taken aback and jumped out of his chair.

"Listen!"

Tom listened, too shocked to speak and heard the faint sound of an engine, getting louder each second, but it didn't sound like a car.

"Right on time. Just the way I like it." The Conductor smiled a lopsided smile which further unnerved Tom, pressed another button on his remote and a door opened behind him.

Chapter 20 – An Unexpected Invitation

"Come with me, Tom," the Conductor said in a way which suggested he was used to telling people what to do rather than asking them. He pushed his chair back, stood up and walked towards the open door.

"Where are we going?" Tom stood up nervously.

The sound of the engine became louder and a sudden gust of wind whooshed through the office, strong enough to ruffle Tom's hair. He closed his eyes against the dust that came with it and blocked his ears with his hands against the noise.

"Your mom is here," the Conductor said as the sound of the engine began to quieten.

Tom opened his eyes again and looked through the door. He could see through to a large courtyard where a beige helicopter had just landed, its blades turning slower and slower and eventually coming to a stop. The helicopter had purple writing on its tail. Purple and beige, just like the carriages of the train, Tom thought. A man dressed in a very smart dark blue suit and cap was opening the back door of the helicopter and Tom could see his mom clambering out.

"How do you get everyone to the destination station so quickly? The train travels for an hour and a half!" Tom said.

"Who said the train goes in a straight line?" the Conductor replied gruffly and continued to walk towards the helicopter.

Tom walked around the desk and outside into the courtyard. The concrete floor was marked out in yellow, three giant circles each with the letter 'H' in the middle. Tom recognised them as helicopter landing pads, from a video game. The courtyard was surrounded by a high brick wall with no other doors.

"Tom, I'm so proud of you! You were amazing! I was so worried when Isabelle was trapped in the cage!" His mom rushed from the helicopter and squeezed him so tight Tom could feel all the air being crushed from him. "I saw every second! You would have loved it! There were loads of screens and hundreds of different camera angles! You could have cut the tension with a knife when you were in the station puzzle."

"Thanks, Mom. You're crushing me a bit though," squeaked Tom.

"Your dad would be so proud."

Out of the corner of his eye, Tom saw the Conductor nod very slightly. "Huh? Dad?" Tom said confused. "Don't you mean Phil?"

Before his mom could answer the Conductor walked up to her and held out his hand. "Ms Treadwell, it's an honor to meet you again." His face seemed to soften as he spoke to her.

"Call me Trudi," said Tom's mom.

"Again? What's going on?"

"So sorry, Trudi. Where are my manners? I was your driver this morning, in disguise. I was keen to meet young Tom here before he went on the train. I had a good feeling about him."

"How did you know where to find us?" She frowned at the Conductor.

The Conductor didn't reply, but gestured Tom and his mom towards the waiting helicopter.

"We're on a tight schedule." The Conductor gestured to the open door of the helicopter. "And I don't like to be late."

He avoided that question again, thought Tom, but the pull of flying was too much for him.

"Are we really going in a helicopter? That's so awesome!" Tom rushed over to where the pilot was still holding the door open and clambered inside.

Trudi and the Conductor walked over to the helicopter. "Did my team explain everything to you, Trudi?"

"Yes, they did. I can't thank you enough. I phoned Phil and explained it to him."

"You're welcome. After you." He indicated with his hand for Trudi to enter the helicopter before him, where the man with the smart blue suit was still patiently holding the door open. The Conductor climbed in after her.

"Thank you, Gary," he said as Gary closed the door behind him and climbed into the front seat next to the pilot, who was also wearing a smart dark blue suit and cap.

"Come on, let's go!" called Tom from inside the helicopter. He had never been so excited. "Where are we going?" As he watched Gary fasten his seat belt he saw the controls, switches, dials and levers. "Are we going home? I can't wait to see the neighbors faces when we pull up on the drive in a helicopter."

"No, Tom," said Trudi. "Seat belt on."

"Hey, wow! Mr. Pilot, what do all those switches do? And that button? How high do we go? How fast?"

"Put your seat belt on, mister. Or we're going nowhere. And no more questions."

"How long are we going for?" Tom couldn't help himself asking one final question.

"You won't miss school on Monday, if that's what you're hoping." Tom's mom laughed. "Now, seat belt on!" she said sternly.

"Good afternoon, sir. Is it the usual destination today?" the pilot said politely to the Conductor when he could finally get a word in between Tom's questions.

"Good afternoon, Ed. Not today. Here's today's destination." The Conductor reached into his inside jacket pocket, pulled out a folded piece of paper and passed it to the pilot.

The pilot looked at it. "Very good, sir. Just a few pre-flight checks to make and then we will be off."

"Thank you, Ed." The Conductor turned to Tom. "Tom, as you know, I have been waiting for a long time for someone to beat my puzzles and now finally you have. I've been working on a new project, something that will eclipse the Puzzle Train. I needed a team worthy of the privilege to be the first to test it."

"But where are we going?" Tom asked again, more impatiently.

The pilot was pressing buttons and flicking switches, and they could hear the rotors begin to turn. Tom felt a tingling in his stomach. He had never been in a helicopter before.

"I have been developing an even bigger adventure, a bigger challenge, bigger puzzles with a longer time limit than the Puzzle Train, Tom. A challenge that took me six years to develop and complete. A challenge that has been ready and waiting for the right team to come along. You have earned the right."

The Conductor paused and looked at Tom, scrutinising him with his dark eyes.

"You will be the first to attempt Puzzle Island!"

Richard James Edwards was born and bred in the Cambridgeshire countryside. Educated in a castle, he became an accountant in Cambridge until destiny took him to South Africa in 2011, where he now lives with his wife.

Puzzle Train is his first novel, but there are lots more to come. Visit him at www.thepuzzletrain.com, find the Puzzle Train on Facebook or email him at thepuzzletrainseries@gmail.com, he would love to hear from you.

Also available – Puzzle Island – ISBN 978-0-620-85646

Coming soon – Puzzle Castle

www.ingramcontent.com/pod-product-compliance
Lightning Source LLC
Chambersburg PA
CBHW051045050726
47592CB00002B/405